Alexander McCall Smith is the author of the bestselling No. 1 Ladies' Detective Agency series. He has written over thirty books for young readers, including two other School Ship *Tobermory* adventures.

Iain McIntosh's illustrations have won awards in the worlds of advertising, design and publishing. He has illustrated many of Alexander McCall Smith's books.

SCHOOL
SHIP
TOBERMORY

Tobermory
ALEXANDER McCALL SMITH
SCHOOL SHIP TOBERMORY
ILLUSTRATIONS BY
IAIN McINTOSH
BC

This edition published in 2017 by
BC Books,
an imprint of Birlinn Limited
West Newington House
10 Newington Road
Edinburgh
EH9 1QS

www.birlinn.co.uk
Reprinted 2018
First published in hardback in 2015

ISBN: 978 1 78027 343 3

British Library Cataloguing-in-Publication Data
A catalogue record for this book is available
from the British Library

Typeset by Mark Blackadder

Printed and bound by
Grafica Veneta, Italy
www.graficaveneta.com

THIS BOOK
is for
NILES
KINDER

ATLANTIC OCEAN
Mainland of Scotland
Tobermory
SOUND OF MULL
ISLE OF MULL
CAPITAL: TOBERMORY
AND HOME PORT OF
SCHOOL SHIP
TOBERMORY
N
W
E
S
0 12 km
0 6 miles

A very unusual school

"Ready?" asked Fee's father. "Are you ready to bring us up?"

Fee nodded. She had sat at the controls of the family submarine many times before this, but you know how it is when somebody asks you to take over a submarine – you always feel just a little bit nervous.

"Yes," she said, trying her best to sound brave. "I'm ... I'm sort of ready."

Both Fee and her twin brother, Ben, had been taught from a very early age to help sail the submarine belonging to their parents, who were well-known marine scientists. Now, at twelve, almost thirteen, Fee had enough experience to bring the vessel up to the surface all by herself. But it was a very big responsibility, and it always brought to mind the things that could go wrong.

What if you made a mistake and dived instead of surfacing? What if you surfaced too quickly, so that the submarine popped up out of the sea like a cork out of water? What if you came up right underneath a large ship – a massive oil tanker, perhaps – broke the glass observation window and then went straight down again? There were so many things that could go wrong in a submarine.

"Right," said her father. "Take her up, Fee! You'll do fine, of course, but I'll be in the engine room if you need me."

Once her father had left the control room she was quite alone. Her brother was doing his packing in his cabin, and her mother was busy in the galley – the submarine's tiny kitchen – making sandwiches for the twins. Fee was by herself. Entirely.

Slowly she pulled the control column towards her. She could not see exactly where she was going – that's never easy in a submarine – but she hoped there was nothing ahead of them, or above. The last thing a submarine wants to meet is a whale or a rock – or a whale *and* a rock, for that matter. You have to hope, too, that there isn't another submarine coming up for air in exactly the same place as you.

A few minutes later, when they were just below the surface, Ben entered the control room.

"I've finished my packing," he announced. "What about you?"

She glanced at her brother. She could see that he was excited, but she had far more important things to do than talk about packing.

"You mustn't disturb me," she said. "I'm just about to look through the periscope."

He became quiet. It is always a special moment when you raise a submarine's periscope, because that is when you find out where you are. You hope that you have come up in the right place, but you can never be absolutely sure. So if your hands shake a little as the periscope rises above the waves, and if you feel your heart thump a bit more loudly, then that is entirely normal.

Fee peered into the periscope as she pushed it

upwards. There was water, just water, swirling round in every direction, and then, with no warning at all, she saw sunlight. The periscope was above the surface.

"What can you see?" Ben asked.

She blinked. The light was very intense and it would take a moment for her eyes to adjust.

You can turn a periscope round, so that it gives you a view in every direction. She would do that – just to check that nothing was coming – but first she would have a good look at the land.

"I can see an island in the distance," she said. "I can see the shore."

Ben caught his breath. "That'll be Mull," he said. Mull was the island they were heading for.

"It's sunny," said Fee. "It's morning."

"And Tobermory?" asked Ben. "Can you see Tobermory?"

"Which Tobermory?" asked Fee. "Tobermory the town or *Tobermory* the ship?"

She was right to ask: there were two Tobermorys. Tobermory, the town, was where the *Tobermory*, the ship, was based. They were going to the *Tobermory*, the ship, but Tobermory, the place, was the harbour in which she (and ships are always called *she*) was normally anchored. The *Tobermory* was a sailing ship and a school at the same time. It was a boarding school on the sea, and while most schools stay in exactly the same place all the time, this one did not.

This one sailed about, teaching everybody not only subjects like history and science – the things that normal schools teach – but also everything that you needed to know if you were going to be a sailor.

"I can't see either of them," said Fee. "I think we might be a little way away. But we can't be too far."

"Let me have a look," said Ben, sounding rather impatient. Although they were twins, Fee had been born two minutes before her brother, and that made her older. It was only two minutes, but she often said that those two minutes were very important. "When you've been alive two minutes longer than somebody else," she was fond of saying, "it shows. You're just a bit more grown-up, you see."

Ben did not look at it that way. He thought he was every bit as mature as his sister, and felt entitled to do everything she did. Right then he felt that he should have a turn on the periscope. "Let me look," he repeated.

"No," she said. "I've spotted a seagull. Oh, it's come down lower. I think it's going to land on top of the periscope!"

Fee laughed as she watched the seagull land. She had a good view of its yellow feet. As she watched, it flapped its wings, sending little droplets of water splashing against the outer lens of the periscope.

Slowly she moved the periscope round, so that she could look in other directions. The seagull did not like this, and flapped its wings again in protest. Then she saw it.

"There's a boat coming straight towards us!" she cried out.

"Dive!" shouted Ben.

Because his sister was busy pulling down the periscope, Ben decided to take the controls himself. Pushing the column forwards, he opened the throttle as far as he could. The submarine responded immediately, giving a lurch downwards.

It was just in time. Seconds later they heard the thud of a boat's engine pass directly over them.

"You should have looked round you," accused Ben. "You should have looked instead of watching that seagull." Although he was very fond of his sister, Ben secretly liked it when she did something to remind her she was not perfect.

Fee looked crestfallen. "I'm sorry," she said. But then she said, rather crossly, "We can all make mistakes, you know."

"Is everything all right?" their mother called out from the galley. "I felt a bit of a lurch there."

"Everything's fine," shouted Ben in reply. He could have said, 'Fee didn't spot a boat coming straight at us!' But he did not. He could have added, 'And I had to take over the controls to get us out of trouble!' But again he did not. Instead of this he simply said, "We're going up again," and left it at that.

They surfaced once more, and this time they were both able to have a good look through the periscope. Fee had been right – they were not far from the island – but they were also closer than she had thought to both Tobermorys. There was the town, a small harbour with brightly painted houses curving round the rim of the bay. There were people walking down the street, off to buy their newspapers and their morning bread and milk. And there in the harbour, riding proudly on its great anchor chain, was the most remarkable sailing ship they had ever seen. And across its bow was the name painted in shining blue paint – *SCHOOL SHIP TOBERMORY*.

"I think it's safe to go all the way up now," said Ben.

Fee guided the submarine right up to the surface. Now they could open the hatches and step out onto the deck to gaze at the ship that was to be their new home. As Fee stared at the *Tobermory* through the submarine's binoculars, she felt no qualms about joining the school. She had always tried not to be frightened by new experiences – nor by the dark, nor bad dreams, nor the thought of what could go wrong. *That'll soon be me,* she thought, as she studied the distant figures on the ship's deck. Although she could not make out what they were doing, they all seemed busy.

It was a wonderful sight. The great ship was painted white from bow to stern. Along the side were lines of neat portholes – the windows of a ship. And, as he stood next to his sister, gazing over at the *Tobermory*, Ben thought about how one of the portholes would soon be his to look out of.

It was a very exciting thought, even if it made him feel just a little bit anxious. He had never been away from family for any length of time, and although people told him that going away to school was fun he was not sure whether it would be fun for him. What would it be like sharing everything with a lot of people you didn't know? Could you be sure they wouldn't laugh at you if you did something stupid? What if you lost your toothbrush, or your pyjamas, or one of your socks? What if somebody came and pushed you around or stole your money?

He had wanted to ask Fee some of these questions, but she had seemed so confident about what lay ahead that he had been unable to do so.

"What will it be like?" was all he had managed.

And she replied, "It's going to be great." And then, after a short pause, "You're not scared, are you?"

He shook his head. "No, I'm not scared. Of course I'm not scared." That is what people who are scared often say.

"Good," said Fee. "Because I'm not going to be able to look after you all the time, you know."

She did not say that unkindly, but it did not really help Ben very much. He wondered why she had thought she would have to look after him. Did she know something he did not? Had she heard things about the *Tobermory* that he had missed? But this was not the time for such thoughts. They had the ship to look at, and now, as the submarine sailed a bit closer, they were able to make out more details.

Above the ship, towering to what seemed like an impossible height, were the masts. The *Tobermory* was a sailing ship, and it had masts from which sails were suspended. These sails would fill with wind when a breeze blew up, and it is this that would drive the ship through the water. The ship also had an engine, of course, that it could use to go in and out of harbour or to help it on its way if there was no wind, but for most of the time it would rely on its sails.

"Look at all those ropes," marvelled Fee, pointing to what looked like an elaborate web spun by some giant spider.

Ben shielded his eyes from the sun to get a better view. "That's the rigging. Those ropes keep the masts in place."

"And you climb up them?" It all seemed very high to Fee.

"Yes," said Ben, taking his turn with the binoculars. "I've seen pictures of people doing that."

Although they had spent a lot of time on their parents' submarine – sometimes weeks and weeks at a stretch – Fee and Ben had never been on a sailing

ship. That had not stopped them, though, from applying for a place on board the school ship, encouraged by their parents, who had decided that the *Tobermory* was just the right school for them. They had needed to think about boarding school for Ben and Fee as they were often away on research expeditions. Up to then, the twins had stayed with an aunt who looked after them while their parents were away, but this was going to be much more difficult, as the aunt had found a job that involved travel.

They had looked at various schools, but had not really liked what they saw. One was in a remote place on a mountainside and appeared dark and uncomfortable. The dormitory floors, they noticed, were all at an angle, with the result that the beds followed the slope of the mountainside. Sleeping in such a bed, thought Fee, would be most peculiar, as your toes would be much lower than your head, and all your blood would end up in your feet. And the blankets would gradually slip down to the end of the bed, which would mean that your top half would be too cold and your lower half too warm. "Not for you, I think," said their mother – much to their relief.

Then there was the school that made everyone take a cold shower every morning. "It's very character-building," explained the principal.

"And very freezing," said their mother – to suppressed giggles from Fee and Ben.

That same principal believed in lots of physical activity – all the time. So, as people moved from classroom to classroom they all ran, and meals were eaten standing up, so that people could do push-ups and other exercises between courses.

"It all helps to build people up," said the principal proudly.

Then somebody suggested the *Tobermory*, and their parents had remembered meeting the captain when he had once berthed his ship near their submarine. "He's a very kind man," remarked Mrs MacTavish, who wanted the best for her twins. "You'll be happy there. I've heard good things about that ship."

"Such as?" asked Ben. The idea of going away to school was still new to him.

"Just good things in general," his mother replied. "Good things like making friends, which you've always wanted. And other things too ..." She did not explain further, but just waved her hand and said, "You'll find out."

His mother was trying to reassure him, thought Ben, but did she really know what life would be like on the *Tobermory*?

"That's right," said Fee, who had overheard this conversation. "You'll find out."

But she, too, did not know, thought Ben.

Their father nosed the submarine in as close to the *Tobermory* as he thought safe.

"You'll have to paddle the rest of the way in your dinghy," he explained. "We'll wave goodbye from here."

Ben and Fee began to blow up the inflatable boat that had been a present for their last birthday. It was not very big, but it would have just enough room to carry them both, together with their kitbags. They had been told not to bring a suitcase, but rather to bring luggage that could be folded and put into a locker. Now their two full kitbags, both labelled with their names, Ben and Fee MacTavish, stood at the ready on top of the submarine.

Once the boat was inflated, Ben pushed it gently from the submarine deck and into the water. Their mother, coming up from below, pressed two packets of sandwiches into their hands. "You might feel hungry before lunch," she said. "I've heard the school food's very good on the *Tobermory*, but just in case ..."

They thanked her, and she gave them each a goodbye kiss, as did their father.

"I know you're going to be all right," said their mother. "But I'll be thinking of you. Will you think of me too? Every day?"

They both reassured her that they would.

"And you will write, won't you?" she said. "It doesn't have to be a long letter – even a postcard will do."

"Of course we will," said Fee.

"We'll be back to collect you at the end of term," Fee's father said.

"Work hard," said Mrs MacTavish. "And remember to clean your teeth after every meal – *every* meal, please. And don't forget to floss!"

"Yes, yes," said Ben. He was eager to make the short crossing to their new home and he had decided to be brave. He could see that already there were other people on the deck of the sailing ship – people in smart blue uniforms swabbing the decks from buckets of sea water, polishing brass fittings, and generally looking very busy. These would be his new schoolmates – his new friends, he hoped. He was eager to meet them.

They climbed down into the boat and set off.

"Goodbye!" shouted their mother, waving a handkerchief.

"Goodbye!" they both shouted, as they started to paddle their way across the short stretch of water.

As they reached the side of the great sailing ship, Fee and Ben both turned round to have one last look at their parents. But their mother and father had disappeared back into the submarine, and now the dark tube of the vessel was beginning to sink below the surface of the sea. They waved, although they knew that their parents would not be able to see them. They felt sad to be saying goodbye, and both of them now felt a bit anxious, but when you are starting at a new school there is no time to think too much about the family you have left behind. This is especially true when your new school is towering above you and somebody is lowering a rope ladder for you to climb up. Not everybody starts school that way, but Ben and Fee did.

"Tie your dinghy to this rope," shouted somebody from above them. "Then, once you've climbed up the rope ladder, we'll pull your boat up too."

A rope came snaking down from above. Fee tied this to the rubber boat, stowed the paddles safely, and then she and Ben began to inch their way up the rope ladder.

"Ben," whispered Fee as they began the climb. "Aren't you just a little bit … scared?"

Ben, who had started first, looked down at his sister beneath him. His decision to be brave was working. "Don't be scared, Fee," he said. "I'm not."

But she was. And so would anybody be. The water seemed a long way down below now, and the *Tobermory* was rocking in the swell of the sea, making the rope ladder swing out from the side of the ship.

"I didn't hear you," said Fee. "What did you say?"

"I said I'm not scared," repeated Ben.

And oddly enough, simply saying that he was not scared seemed to help.

They were nearly at the top of the ladder now, and he even managed to smile as he saw a pair of hands stretch out over the railings to help him clamber onto the deck. Ben looked up and saw that the hands belonged to a boy of about his own age, dressed in a smart blue uniform and grinning at him in a friendly way. The boy had a cheerful look to him – the sort of look that makes you think, *I hope he'll be my friend.*

"I'm Badger Tomkins," said the boy as he gripped Ben's wrists and pulled him onto the deck. "Who are you?"

"I'm Ben," said Ben.

"I was told to look out for you," said Badger.

"Welcome aboard the *Tobermory*!"

Badger now turned to help Fee. "You must be Fee," he said. "I saw your name on the list of new students. Welcome, Fee!"

"What do we do now?" asked Ben.

"We haul up your dinghy," said Badger. "Then we let the air out of it and stow it away. Everything has to be stowed away neatly on the ship. It's one of the rules."

"Are there lots of rules?" asked Ben.

Badger laughed. "Plenty," he said. "Maybe five or six hundred. But don't worry. You probably only need to know ten. Those are called the big rules. All the others are called small rules, and we don't pay much attention to them."

Fee stared at Badger. "Do you like it here?" she asked.

Badger thought this a rather odd question. "But of course I like it," he answered. "This is the most amazing, fantastic, exciting, superb, ace school in … in the entire world."

"Are you joking?" asked Ben.

"Not at all," said Badger. "You'll see soon enough." He paused. "Mind you, I won't pretend that there aren't some things that aren't so great."

"What are those?" asked Ben.

"You'll see," said Badger again. He looked at his watch. "We'd better get your boat up. Breakfast is in half an hour and if you're late all the sausages will be taken." He made a face. "Some people always try to take more than their fair share."

"Who are they?" asked Fee.

"You'll see," said Badger once again. "But let's not stand about talking. Let's get the boat up and then I can take you to the Captain before breakfast. We always have to take new people to the Captain when they arrive."

"Is he the principal?" asked Ben.

"He is," said Badger. "But you never call him that. He's called the Captain because he's the captain of the ship. His full name is Captain Macbeth. He's also a teacher, of course, but his main job is running the ship."

They began to haul up their dinghy. Once it was up on deck, they took out the plug, deflated it, and stowed it away in a nearby locker. The locker was full of other dinghies, all folded up just as theirs was. "This is where we keep our personal boats," explained Badger. "Mine is that red one over there. It has a bit of a leak, I'm afraid, but I don't use it often now. We have a class in the care and maintenance of rubber boats. They teach you how to stick a plaster over any holes."

Badger looked at his watch again. "Right," he said. "Ready for the Captain? Yes? Well, in that case follow me!"

A meeting with the Captain

"This way," said Badger, picking his way across the deck. "Mind you don't trip on those coils of rope."

There was a lot going on. Here and there on the ship's wide deck there were groups of people attending to various tasks. Some were washing the decks with buckets of water hauled up over the ship's side, some were polishing brass railings, while others were sorting out kitbags piled up near one of the hatches.

"It's always like this at the start of a new term," remarked Badger. "There's a lot to do before we go out to sea."

A boy rushed past Badger, greeting him as he ran off on some errand. "Hi, Badge," he called out, and then, "Got to go!"

Badger gave him a smart salute. "That's the Head Prefect of the Lower Deck," he said. "We have three decks, you see, where everybody lives. He's my friend."

Fee and Ben felt a little bit overwhelmed. Everybody looked so busy – and also seemed so confident of their tasks. By contrast, neither of them had any idea what to do. It was all very well being used to submarines, but it seemed that a sailing ship was quite different. Submarines had very few ropes, and no sails of course. And their family submarine was so small beside this great ship that seemed to go on forever in every direction.

Badger was walking quickly, and Ben and Fee had to struggle to catch up with him.

"You don't sound Scottish," said Ben. "Where are you from?"

"Oh, we're all from all over the place," Badger answered. "I'm American. I come from New York. But the school has people from everywhere, really. Poppy, over there, is from Australia. You'll like her, by the way. She's also my friend."

He pointed to a tall girl with red hair, who caught his eye and waved.

"If you live in New York," Ben asked, "then why are you at school over here?"

Badger frowned. "It's a long story," he said. "My parents, you see, are very busy. They work all the time."

"In one of those tall buildings?"

"Yes," said Badger. "On the forty-fifth floor. And I'm afraid they're too busy to spend much time with me. They wanted to send me to a boarding school in the woods in a place called Vermont. But you know something? I don't really like trees all that much. I much preferred the idea of going to a school where you can do sailing. So I did some research and found out about the *Tobermory*. I had to persuade them – which wasn't easy – but eventually they agreed. So here I am." He paused. "I don't think they really notice whether or not I'm around."

Ben was not sure what to say. His own parents had not sent him away because they were too busy – they always had a lot of time for him – and for Fee, too. They were at boarding school because it was difficult to get to school if you spent a lot of time on a submarine, and of course there was also the problem of their aunt's new job.

He decided that the best thing to say to Badger was "I'm sorry." You can never go far wrong if you say you're sorry.

"That's all right," said Badger. "I'm used to it. And maybe one day they'll stop being busy and we'll be able to do some stuff together." He paused. "You know what I'd really like to do? I'd like to go sailing with them again. We did that once, and I really liked it – just sailing with my Mom and Dad."

"I hope you do," said Fee.

They had now reached a set of steps a bit like a ladder that led down from the deck into the inside

of the ship. "These steps are called the companionway," said Badger. "That's something you need to remember. Just about everything on a ship has a special name, and you're going to have to remember that. If you call things by the wrong name three times in a row you can end up on potato-peeling duty."

"Oh," said Fee. They never bothered with the names of things on the submarine. She had always simply said "that thingy over there" or "that funny-looking handle" and "that red what-do-you-call-it?" But what was this warning about potato-peeling?

"They make you peel potatoes?" she asked.

"Yes," said Badger. "That's the main punishment round here. That, and extra scrubbing of the deck,

but you have to do something really bad to get that. The worst thing that can happen to you, though, is to be made to clean out the bathrooms. We call those the *heads*, by the way – we never say bathroom on a ship."

"I hope that we don't have to …" began Fee.

"Oh, don't worry," said Badger. "It's not a strict school. The Captain is kind and the teachers are fine too. You're not going to be unhappy, you know. We all love this place."

They made their way down the companionway. It was rather dark down below, as the only place for light to get in was through the portholes on the side of the ship. But their eyes quickly became used to the darkness, and they could make out that they were in a passageway at the end of which was a large wooden door.

"That's the Great Cabin," said Badger. "It's the Captain's office, but it's also the place where he hangs his hammock and has some of his meals."

"What's he like?" whispered Ben as they approached the door.

Badger paused before he knocked. "The Captain? Oh, you'll like him. He's a large man, and he has a beard. But a lot of the teachers have beards – the men teachers, that is. The women teachers all wear their hair in a ponytail, except Matron, who is an excellent high diver, and has her hair cut short so that it doesn't get in her eyes when she's diving."

"What do we call him?" asked Fee. "Do we have to call him sir?"

Badger shook his head. "You can if you want, but mostly we call him Captain," he said. "And he'll call you by your name, or, if he forgets that, he'll call you *sailor*. The teachers usually call us by our names, except for the ship's cook, who's married to Matron, and who calls everybody 'you', except for me: he calls me Badger because I think he likes me. And Matron, of course – he calls her 'Rabbit', which makes us want to laugh. But we don't, of course, because the ship's cook is in charge of how much ice cream we get and if he gets cross with you, then you get a tiny portion of ice cream instead of a normal one. So, never laugh at the ship's cook. That's what we call an important rule."

Badger reached forward to knock. Almost immediately a voice called out from inside and Badger opened the door. The Great Cabin was before them, and there, behind a large desk on which charts were spread out in confusion, sat the Captain of the *Tobermory*.

"Well, well, well," said the Captain. "Now who do we have here?"

"They're new," said Badger. "They've just arrived. We've stowed their boat already."

"Well done," said the Captain. "Now you wait outside, Badger, so that I can talk to these two fine young people."

Badger left, closing the door behind him. Ben and Fee stood in front of the Captain's desk, both feeling a bit nervous. They were relieved, though, to see the Captain had a kind face and that he smiled as he talked to them.

"You must be Ben and Fee MacTavish," began the Captain. "You're both very welcome aboard the *Tobermory*!"

"Thank you, Captain," said Ben, trying hard to sound confident.

The Captain nodded. "I met your parents once, you know. It was a few years ago when they were on

their submarine up near Iceland. They were tracking seals, I think, for some big scientific project."

"They told us that," said Fee. "We were staying with our aunt then."

"You must have done quite a bit of sea time," said the Captain.

Ben hesitated, but then said, "We're not really experienced, Captain. We've been on our parents' submarine a lot, but it's completely different. You don't get to know the sea so well when you're under it."

The Captain thought about this. "Yes, I suppose so. You never see the waves, do you? And you never need to bother about the wind."

"So we don't really know much about sailing ships," said Fee.

"I see," said the Captain. "Well, we'll set that right." He paused, and looked at them intently. "So, here you are, right at the beginning of your time on the *Tobermory*. And I have to ask you something. I ask everybody this question when they first come to us. I make no exceptions."

They waited for the question.

"This is what I need to ask," said the Captain, looking first into Fee's eyes and then into Ben's. "Do you really want to be sailors? Do you really want that, deep down in your heart? Because if you don't, you know, then it's best to stop right here. I won't think any the less of you if you tell me you don't want to go to sea. There's a perfectly good shore school in Tobermory itself and they'll take you, if you prefer to be on dry land."

Ben glanced at Fee, and she shook her head. "No," he said. "This is what we want. We really want to go to sea."

The Captain smiled. "Very well. But I must tell you one other thing, and it's a very important thing. Going to sea can be dangerous. As a member of this school you will face challenges that people who go to school on land never have to face. There will be times when we shall all be in danger – I can guarantee you that. Are you prepared for that?"

This time it was Fee who glanced at Ben. He did not hesitate to nod. And so Fee said to the Captain, "My brother and I are both prepared to face danger, Captain. We promise you that."

The Captain rubbed his hands together. "That's the spirit! So all you have to do now is find your berths. Mind you, you don't really have a berth as such, as you will be sleeping in hammocks. But Badger will show you. Girls have their cabins on the starboard side – that means the right-hand side – and boys on the port side – that's the left-hand side. But of course you'll know that already from being on your parents' submarine."

Fee swallowed hard. She had heard those terms before, but she always found it difficult to remember which was which.

"And you can get your kit from Matron," the Captain continued. "She'll give you a toothbrush and a towel and things like that. Understood?"

The Captain called out for Badger, who quickly reappeared from behind the door.

"Matron first," barked the Captain. "Then Middle Deck." Badger nodded. "Aye, aye. I'll take them right away, Captain."

Once outside the Great Cabin, Badger turned to Ben and said, "I'm glad you're on Middle Deck. It's the best place to be. I'm there. And Poppy too. It's the best deck on the whole ship."

Matron's a diver

"Matron's cabin," said Badger, "is one deck below, on the starboard side." He looked at Ben and Fee. "That means: on the right-hand side of the ship as you face the front."

Fee nodded. She was beginning to pick up the special nautical words. "Starboard right, port left," she muttered. And then added, "And the floor's …"

"The deck," prompted Badger. "Well done, Fee!" To get there from the Great Cabin they had to make their way along a narrow passageway, and it was there that they saw the dog. They could easily have missed him, though, as he was not very big and was scurrying along rather quickly, with the air of a dog who knows exactly where he is going.

"That's the Captain's dog," explained Badger. "His name is Henry and he's quite useful. He carries things around. If you give him a piece of rope and say, 'Take that to the Captain, Henry,' he'll do just that. As long as you use his name, that is. If you forget to say 'Henry' he'll just stare at you and do nothing. He's particular about manners."

Henry disappeared round a corner.

"He looks busy," said Ben.

"He often is at the beginning of term," said Badger. "But then when we're out at sea he doesn't have quite so much to do. You often find him standing by one of the railings, staring down at the water or looking out to sea."

Badger paused before continuing, "There's a strange story about him. Would you like to hear it?"

Ben said that they would, and so the three of them squatted down in the passageway as Badger told them

the story. "I'm not sure if this really happened," he began, "but I'll tell you anyway. I think it may be true, but on the other hand it may not. It's difficult to say."

"We don't mind," said Ben. "Please tell us the story."

"Right," began Badger. "Henry was up on the deck one morning. He was on watch, which means he was on duty. You'll find out all about that. You go on watch for about four hours, then once you've done that you're not on watch for the rest of the day."

"What do you do when you're on watch?" asked Fee.

"You watch," replied Ben. "You have to look out and see that the ship doesn't bump into anything. You also have to take your turn at the helm – that's the steering wheel – and so on."

"We steer the ship?" asked Ben, amazed at the thought of being in charge of so large a boat. Like Fee, he had taken a turn at steering the family submarine, but that was so much smaller than the *Tobermory*.

"Oh yes," said Badger. "You get used to it, although when you're still new – which you are, of course – you have to be extra careful. There was a boy once who almost took us onto the rocks because he was gazing up at the clouds when he should have been looking where we were going. And there was a girl who took us in a complete circle because she was talking on her phone at the time. The Captain doesn't like that sort of thing, you know."

This reminded Fee of what had happened the last time she had brought the submarine to the surface. "Oops," she said. "I feel sorry for that girl. I know how easy it is to be distracted …"

"By looking at seagulls, for instance," said Ben, giving his sister a sideways glance. "Sorry, Fee, maybe I shouldn't have said that."

Badger, though, was interested to hear about the incident. "What happened?" he asked.

"I'm afraid it was my fault," said Fee. "I was looking through the periscope and a seagull landed on top of it. I was studying its feet while I should have been turning the periscope round to see if we were in any danger."

"And we were," said Ben.

"A ship was coming straight at us," said Fee. "Fortunately we managed to dive in time."

"Things happen very quickly at sea," said Badger. "One moment everything's fine and then, before you know it, you're in real danger."

"Tell us about Henry," urged Ben.

"Right," said Badger. "So Henry was on watch with a couple of people and was looking out to sea. We weren't moving fast as there was hardly any wind in the sails. We were just drifting, I suppose, and we weren't too far off the shore of the Isle of Skye, which is just round the corner from here.

"Everybody who wasn't on watch was having a lesson in knot-tying at the time and so nobody really saw what happened next, apart from the boy at the helm, and he was a bit vague about it later.

"Anyway, apparently Henry saw something on the shore and started to bark. Then, before anybody could stop him, he dived off the deck and into the water. He had seen Matron diving, you see, and must have picked it up from her. Then he swam towards the shore and there was a lot of splashing before he turned round to swim back. But do you know what? He had something in his paws."

"He'd caught a fish?" asked Fee.

Badger shook his head. "No, it wasn't a fish, although it looked quite like one." He paused. "It was a mermaid!"

Fee gasped.

"Surely not!" said Ben. "Mermaids don't really exist, do they?"

Badger shrugged. "I'm just telling you the story. I'm just telling you what people told me."

"Carry on," said Fee. Ben was always saying that things didn't exist, and she felt that if you said that all the time there would be no point in having any stories at all.

"Well," went on Badger, "they pulled him up on to the deck and the mermaid came with him. She wasn't pleased, apparently, and a bit cold too. Somebody lent her a jacket and they gave her a cup of soup to warm her up. Henry looked quite proud that he had caught a mermaid, but the Captain was cross with him and told him to go down to his cabin. He has a very small cabin – not much bigger than a shoebox, near the bilges."

Fee interrupted him. "The bilges?" It was another of these special words.

"The bilges are right down at the bottom of the ship," explained Badger. "They're a special compartment where any water that gets in will be collected. They're usually a bit smelly, and dark too. I wouldn't like to go down there alone."

Badger resumed his story. "So Henry went down rather reluctantly, his tail between his legs, while everybody looked at the mermaid."

"She finished her soup and said something, although nobody knew what it meant. It was a sort of bubbly sound, people said. It was probably 'Thank you'. Then she slithered off the deck – mermaids can't walk, you see – plopped into the sea, and swam off. And that's it. That's the story of Henry and the mermaid. And that's why you see him looking over the railings so much, especially if we're anywhere near Skye. He's looking for that mermaid or another mermaid."

"What an amazing story," said Fee. She hoped

that mermaids existed – even if they did not – as a world with mermaids seemed far more interesting than a world without them.

"Yes," said Badger, looking at his watch. "But we'd better get on, as we have to see Matron, and breakfast is in exactly ten minutes."

Ben and Fee liked Matron the moment they saw her. She shook hands with each of them and gave them a small toffee. "A toffee before breakfast always helps to start the day," she said with a smile. "Now, here is your kit – all bundled up nicely and ready to be taken off to your cabins. Socks, shirts, and so on. Pyjamas. Toothbrush. Toothpaste – I'm afraid toothpaste always tastes a bit salty at sea, but you'll quickly get used to it. Lifejacket. Whistle. Deck shoes. Any questions?"

Ben and Fee shook their heads.

"Now let me give you a quick medical examination," said Matron. "Open your mouths wide, please, and show me your teeth."

They did as they were told, and Matron shone a light into their mouths.

"That all looks satisfactory," she said. "Now show me your hands."

They held out their hands and turned them over. "Good," said Matron. "All your fingers seem to be there."

The Captain's dog, Henry, had something in his paw. What on earth could it be?
TOBERMORY
Once on deck, the mermaid was given a jacket and a mug of soup to warm her up. Mermaids don't like being out of the water ...
Sometimes Henry would stare out to sea for hours, hoping to see another mermaid ...

Then she tapped their heads gently with a rubber hammer. "Nothing wrong there," she said.

And that was it.

"Off to breakfast," said Matron.

They picked up their bundles of kit and started to leave. Ben noticed a framed photograph on the cabin wall and stopped in front of it. The picture showed a woman standing on a high diving board, with a great crowd watching from down below.

Matron spotted his interest. "Yes," she said, "that's me, at the Olympics. I hoped to win a medal, but I didn't. The dive went wrong and I made the most terrible splash. It soaked the judges, I'm afraid. They were absolutely dripping wet."

"Oh dear," said Fee. "What bad luck."

"Everybody laughed," said Matron. "Including me. But the judges didn't think it very funny and gave me no points. I didn't mind. I knew I could dive rather well."

"Will you show us some time?" asked Fee.

"Show you?" asked Matron. "Of course I shall. In fact, I'll teach you, if you like."

Fee had been smiling, but now her face fell. She had always wanted to dive, but each time she had tried it had not been a success. Whenever she went to a swimming pool she would climb up the ladder to the high board, stand at the end, and look down. She would put her hands together, just as you were meant to do, and then, right at the last moment, she would jump rather than dive. It happened every time.

"I'd like that," she said. "I don't think I'm much good, though. I usually flop, not dive!"

Matron laughed. "I think you might surprise yourself," she said. "We'll start some time soon – as long as the sea's not too cold."

They thanked Matron and joined Badger, who was waiting to show them to their cabins.

"We'll have to hurry now," he said. "I'm getting hungry and I can already smell breakfast."

Ben sniffed at the air. There were lots of smells: salt, rope, a touch of tar – things that were new to him. But there was another, familiar smell – that of sizzling sausages.

All the ship's meals were served in the mess hall. This was a large space, as broad as the ship itself, furnished with fifteen long tables, each large enough to seat ten people. Ben noticed immediately that there was something unusual about these tables. Most tables stand on four legs, but these ones were suspended on ropes, making them look like giant swings in a park.

"Look," he said as they reached the door. "Hanging tables!"

"Yes," said Badger. "And there's a reason for that, you know. If the ship tilts over – and it does that a lot, I can tell you – the tables don't tip. And you'll see that the benches are attached to them, too, so that they move as well."

"Just like a swing," said Fee.

Badger nodded. "It's much better this way. If you've ever been on a rough sea you'll know what happens – everything slips and slides about. One moment you can be eating your corn flakes and the next your bowl is upside down on the floor – or in your lap."

Ben looked about. There were already a good number of people in the mess hall, most of them seated at a table. Some, though, were still lined up at the galley hatch.

"That's where we go," said Badger, pointing. "Follow me."

They made their way towards the galley hatch. As they went, both Ben and Fee were aware that many pairs of eyes were on them.

"They're all looking at us," he whispered to Fee. "I wish they wouldn't."

Badger overheard. "Don't worry," he reassured them, "They always stare at new people. It's just for the first day – nobody will notice you tomorrow."

The smell of sausages was now much stronger, and Ben heard his stomach growl in anticipation. He hadn't had time to eat the sandwiches his mother had given them. As they approached the hatch, they helped themselves to a tray, a plate and cutlery.

Standing on the other side of the food counter was

a tough-looking man, his sleeves rolled up to reveal tattoos of anchors, sailing ships and frolicking whales.

"The ship's cook," whispered Badger, and then, in a louder voice, "Morning, Cook!"

The cook looked at him and grinned. "Morning there, young Badger. And who have you got with you, may I ask?"

Nudged by Badger, Ben replied, "I'm Ben, Cook. I'm new."

"I can see that," said the cook, in a not unfriendly tone. "And you over there? You got a name?"

"I'm Fee, sir," said Fee.

"You don't call me sir," said the cook. "You call me Cook. Sir is for the officers, and I isn't an officer."

"She's new too," said Badger, by way of explanation. "She'll learn, Cook."

"I'm sure she will," said Cook. "We all learns soon enough if we keep our eyes open and our ears free of wax. And if we eats our vegetables too, mark you. We serve healthy food in this school, I'll have you know."

"Except at breakfast," muttered Badger.

"What was that?" snapped the cook. "You say something, Badger?"

"Nothing, Cook. Just clearing my throat."

"All right," said Cook, reaching for a saucepan. "Sausages this morning, with fried potatoes, and bread. Hand over your plates. Look sharp about it."

They passed him their plates, watching wide-eyed as he put four large sausages on each, with a fifth one on Badger's. "This young man needs a bit of building up," he said. "Extra sausage for him. Well deserved, too."

As the cook said this, Fee heard a hissing sound from the table immediately behind them. Half-turning round, she saw that this came from a tall boy with a cruel face and a central parting right through the middle of his slick dark hair. Fee guessed that he had seen the extra sausage being given to Badger and was envious.

Badger had heard too. "Pay no attention," he

whispered to Fee. "I'll tell you about him when we get to our table."

Once they had been given their fried potatoes and bread, they made their way to a table at the other end of the dining area. Fee tried not to look at the boy who had been doing the hissing, although she did catch the quickest glimpse of him as they walked past. He was looking directly at her, and their eyes met for the briefest of moments before he transferred his gaze to Ben. At that precise instant, Fee had that extraordinary feeling you have when you know, right down in your bones, that you have made an enemy. You don't need to have done anything to deserve it, but there's no mistaking it when it happens.

The red-haired girl Badger had pointed out earlier was already sitting at their table when they arrived. As they sat down, she looked up from her breakfast and gave them a broad smile, starting with Fee, then moving on to Ben, and finally to Badger. It was the sort of smile that makes you feel warm inside – a smile that says *I'm really glad to see you.*

"So," she said, as she put down her fork. "So you're the new people. You're Ben and Fee, aren't you?"

"That's right," said Badger. "Ben and Fee have just arrived."

"Welcome aboard," said the girl. She smiled again. "My name's Poppy, by the way."

They shook hands.

"I'm from Australia," Poppy said. "I live about as far from the sea as it's possible to get. Right in the middle. The nearest town – and it's not very near, I can tell you – is Alice Springs."

"I've heard of it," said Fee.

"Yes, you will have," said Poppy. "We've got a great big red rock out there. It's called Uluru. It's amazing. People come from all over to take a look at it." She shook her head "Some people get lost out there – you have to be careful."

Ben wondered how Poppy had ended up on the *Tobermory*. "My parents have a big sheep farm," said Poppy. "It's hundreds of miles even from Alice Springs, so I would have to go off to boarding school anyway. I had always been interested in the sea, even though I'd never actually seen it. I had books about it and I think I dreamed about it every single night. Do you know how it is when you really want to do something? You won't be happy until you do it."

Ben nodded. He knew what it was like to want something really badly. He had always wanted to have a friend – a really good friend.

Poppy continued. "So when my parents asked me where I wanted to go, I said I'd heard about a boarding school that was on a ship. They looked it up and ... well, here I am. I've been on the *Tobermory* for two years now, and I've loved every minute of it.

People said to me, 'Oh, you'll be homesick for Australia – you'll want to go home,' but I never felt that. Not once."

She smiled at Ben. "You aren't feeling homesick, are you?"

He was able to answer truthfully that he was not. Well, maybe just a tiny bit. Maybe enough to feel he would like to see his parents just for a little while …

"Feeling homesick is quite normal," Poppy went on. "Lots of people feel a bit that way, but they usually get over it quite quickly. I really like going back to Australia for the holidays and I love being back on the farm, but I always count the days until it's time to come back to the *Tobermory*."

They began their breakfast. The sausages were delicious, and Fee and Ben decided to make them last as long as possible, eating them slowly to savour the taste. Badger ate more quickly, and had soon polished off all five sausages on his plate before starting to tackle the fried bread.

"That boy," he said, his mouth still half full with the last sausage. "That one who hissed."

"Oh him!" said Poppy disdainfully, peering across the row of heads.

"He's called William Edward Hardtack," continued Badger.

"And he's bad news," interjected Poppy.

"Very bad news," said Badger. "We usually just call

him Hardtack. He's the Head Prefect of Upper Deck, and most of the people who sleep up there can't stand him."

"He's a bully," said Poppy. "And he doesn't like Badger. Nor me, for that matter. And we don't like him back. He's a real dingo."

"A dingo's an Australian wild dog," explained Badger. "Poppy often says things like that."

Badger shook his head. "I've never worked out why Hardtack's so mean," he said. "What's the point of being that way?"

"He must think it makes him feel bigger," said Poppy. "Most bullies are like that – they're small people on the inside who want to be big people on the outside."

"Yet his brother wasn't like that," remarked Badger. "Remember him, Poppy? George Churchill Hardtack? He left at the end of last year."

Poppy did remember him. "He was completely different," she mused. "He was really good at everything – swimming, diving, seamanship – everything. But he was kind as well – he'd often help people who weren't so good at things. He once showed me a good way of tying a bowline …"

"That's a really important knot," Badger explained to Ben. "It's the first knot you'll learn – and you must never unlearn it."

"I'll try," said Ben.

Poppy was still thinking about George Churchill Hardtack. "I think that maybe Hardtack couldn't live up to his elder brother – and knew it. Rather than accepting that his brother was better than he was at just about everything – and being proud of him – he became all bitter and twisted." She struggled to think of the right words to explain this. "Like a snake that's got itself all tied up in knots and ends up biting anybody who comes near …"

"And biting itself too," added Badger.

Ben glanced in Hardtack's direction. "And who are the people around him?" he asked.

Badger turned his head to look. When he turned back there was an expression of disgust on his face. "His usual crew," he said. "The thin one on his right is Geoffrey Shark, and the one on his left is Maximilian Flubber. Shark is greedy and tries to grab everything before anybody else gets a chance. He's a thief, I think, but nobody is ever able to prove it. As for Flubber, he'll come over all friendly, but don't trust him – not even for one second. Hardtack has him in his pocket, and anything you say to Flubber goes right back to him."

"Badger's right," agreed Poppy. "Don't believe anything that Flubber says. He's a big liar, although he doesn't know how easy it is to tell when he's lying. His ears move a little – backwards and forwards just a tiny bit – but it always gives the game away."

WILLIAM EDWARD HARDTACK

"Fee saw that the hissing was coming from a tall boy with a cruel face and a central parting right through the middle of his slick dark hair ..."

"The thin one is Geoffrey Shark. Shark is greedy and tries to grab everything before anybody else gets a chance. He's a thief, I think, but nobody is ever able to prove it..."

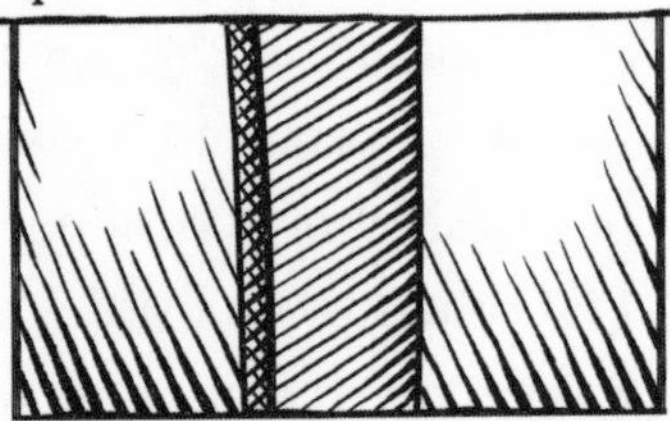

MAXIMILIAN FLUBBER

"As for Flubber, he'll come over all friendly, but don't trust him – not even for one second ..."

Fee felt a bit anxious. Perhaps they should have gone to school on shore after all. "Are they the worst people on the ship?" she asked.

"Yes," said Badger. "Definitely. Most of the others are really nice. It's a friendly ship, but in every group of people, well, you know how it is …"

"He's right," said Poppy. "What's the saying? There are always some rotten apples in the barrel."

"Exactly," said Badger. "But let's not think about them too much. There are far better things to do."

It was at this moment, though, that Ben noticed that William Edward Hardtack had risen from his seat and was walking towards them. He was smiling as he approached, but it was not the sort of smile that would have fooled anyone.

He was soon standing directly behind Ben, who was still seated at the table.

"You're new aren't you?" he said, leaning over Ben's shoulder to shake hands. "I though I'd come and say hello. I wondered whether you were going to be on my deck."

"He isn't," said Badger firmly. "He's on Middle Deck."

"Oh, what a pity," said Hardtack. "Still, it would be nice to shake your hand to welcome you."

Ben took the hand extended to him. It felt cold and dry, and Hardtack's grip was so tight that Ben gave an involuntary wince.

"Oh sorry," said Hardtack. "I always forget that some people don't like a strong handshake."

And then, as the handshake came to an end, Hardtack's hand dropped onto Ben's plate, tipping the two remaining sausages onto the deck.

"Oh, clumsy me!" exclaimed Hardtack. As he said this, he took a step forward. "And look, I've gone and trodden on your sausages. Sorry about that."

"You should be more careful," blurted out Badger.

"Cool it, Striped One," said Hardtack, using the nickname he had made up for Badger. Badgers are striped, of course, but nobody apart from Hardtack and his friends thought this very funny. "An accident's an accident. It's not as if I meant it."

He walked away before Ben had the chance to say anything. On the floor he saw his two squashed sausages. It seemed such a waste – and he was still hungry.

"Here," said Fee. "You can have one of mine."

"And one of mine too," said Poppy.

Badger's eyes narrowed. 'That was no accident," he said. "I've seen him do that before."

Ben tried to make little of it. "I don't care," he said.

"Well I do," muttered Badger.

In deadly peril

Once breakfast was over, Badger and Poppy took their new friends to the Middle Deck to find a hammock and store their belongings.

"Are we going downstairs?" asked Fee, as they left the mess hall.

Poppy gently corrected her. "Not downstairs," she said. "You go downstairs in a building, but in a ship it's *down below*."

Fee blushed. She did not like to be thought of as somebody who had never been to sea – she had been at sea a lot, but in her parents' submarine it was all so different. "On our submarine there's only one deck," she explained. "That's why I'm not used to stairs ..."

Poppy interrupted her. "They aren't stairs," she pointed out. "We call them a companionway or a ladder." She smiled. "Sorry, Fee, but it's best that I tell you."

Fee sighed. "I suppose I'll remember," she said.

Poppy was reassuring. "We all learn soon enough,"

she said. "You'll know everything by ... by tomorrow!"

Fee was not so sure of that, but there was one thing that she was certain about, and that was that she liked Poppy, and Badger too. Having a good friend when you are just starting off on something new always helps, and having two good friends is even better.

Poppy was interested in hearing a bit more about life on a submarine. "It must be pretty cramped down there," she said. "I've seen pictures of submarines, and there's not much room."

"You get used to it," said Fee. "You get used to sharing every bit of space – and not just sharing with people – you share with provisions. We used the space above my bunk to hang sausages and cabbages. And my brother had to share his bunk with a whole lot of tinned tomatoes. It wasn't that comfortable."

Poppy's eyes widened. "And what about air? Did you have enough air?"

"Most of the time," said Fee. "But sometimes when the air supplies got a bit low we had to take it in turns to breathe. I would breathe in when my brother breathed out. Then I would breathe out while he breathed in."

Poppy tried to imagine what that was like. She did not like the sound of taking turns to breathe.

"But that hardly ever happened," Fee went on. "Most of the time we submerged for only a few hours so that my parents could study fish. Then we would surface again and open the hatch to let fresh air in."

While Poppy took Fee to the girls' cabins, Badger led Ben to the boys'. "Here we are," he said, pointing to a door off a passageway. "You can share with me, if you like."

Badger pushed open the door and showed Ben the cabin beyond. It was not big; in fact, Ben thought it rather small. He saw, though, there was enough room for the two hammocks slung from one side of the cabin to the other, and also for a couple of small chests for storage.

"This is my hammock," said Badger. "And that can be yours." He looked enquiringly at Ben. "Have you ever slept in one of these things?"

Ben shook his head. "I've seen hammocks," he said. "But I've never slept in one."

"You'll get used to it quickly," said Badger. "And when the ship's going up and down, you'll be pleased to have a hammock. They swing, you see, like the tables in the mess hall. They're really just swinging beds."

Ben stowed away the clothing he had collected from Matron, and then emptied the kitbag he had brought with him. The chest was just large enough to contain everything, and soon all his possessions were neatly packed away.

"That's it," said Badger, looking at his watch. "And

we're just in time to go back up on deck to report for duty."

It gave Ben a thrill to think that he was reporting for duty. He had never done that before, and he wondered just what his duties would be. It seemed as if Badger had read his mind. "Scrubbing the decks," he said. "Checking the rigging. Polishing the railings. Stowing the boats. Removing the sail covers." He paused. "There are hundreds of things to do before you go to sea, but don't worry. Just stick beside me and do what I do – you can't go wrong that way." He smiled, and then added, "At least, I hope you can't go wrong – though sometimes people do!"

Poppy and Fee were busy uncoiling rope on deck when the two boys emerged. Badger took Ben to a rope ladder that was fastened to the ship's railings at one end and, at the other, to the top of one of the masts. It made Ben dizzy just to look up. Would people really climb all the way up there, he wondered?

His question was answered almost immediately. "I'll show you how to do this," Badger said. "We need to go up and make sure the rigging's secure."

Ben gulped. "All right," he said, trying his hardest to sound confident, but not really succeeding. The rope ladder he had used earlier that day had not seemed to disappear into the clouds, as this one did.

"It's not too bad," said Badger. "All you have to do is to remember not to look down."

Ben thought that was easier said than done. People always tell you not to look down when you're doing something like crossing a narrow bridge over a ravine or climbing up a mountain. *Don't look down*, they say, but of course that is exactly where you want to look, just to check up on how far you would drop if you fell. Not that you are *planning* to fall, of course …

Now they stood at the bottom of the rope ladder. "Would you like to go first?" asked Badger. "If you slip, I'll be able to catch you."

Ben swallowed. He was *not* going to slip. He was *definitely* not going to slip.

But if he did not go first, Badger might think he was afraid, and he did not want that. So he stretched out his arms, gripped one of the rungs, took a deep breath, and began to climb. He felt the ladder move under his weight, and then move again when Badger followed behind him. He took another deep breath and looked up at the climb ahead of him. He suddenly felt surprised: it was not nearly as bad as he had imagined. In fact now he had started he decided that he was actually enjoying himself.

"Are you all right?" Badger called out from beneath him.

"Yes," shouted Ben. "I don't mind this at all."

Badger seemed pleased. "You obviously have a head for heights," he said.

Have I? Ben asked himself. He had never thought about it, but perhaps it was true. Perhaps he was one of those people who can stand on top of a mountain and look down without feeling the slightest bit worried – or one of those window-cleaners who dangle on ropes down the sides of tall buildings and manage to whistle as they work. *I suppose*, he said to himself, *if you don't try things like this you'll never know whether or not you can do them.*

Halfway up the ladder, Ben paused. He knew he should not look down, but he could not help himself. *If I'm going to fall*, he thought, *I might as well know how far it's going to be.* Ever so slowly he turned his head so that he could glance down below him, but quickly he turned it back. It had been an appalling, frightening sight: everything looked so small from up there – the deck, the people standing on it, the coils of rope, the line of life rafts. Even Tobermory harbour and the town, with its moored boats, bobbing in the water, looked small from up there – like a model village by a model bay.

Badger wondered why he had stopped. "Are you all right up there?" he called out.

Ben swallowed hard. He knew that if he was going to stay at this school he would have to get used to this sort of thing. You cannot go to sea feeling frightened of everything. You have to be brave – and he would be.

"Just getting my breath back," he replied. "I'm ready to carry on now."

Hand over hand he made his way up. Foot over foot he climbed the ladder, until a few minutes later he realised that he was at the top. There he stopped and waited for Badger to arrive.

"You need to step out onto the spar," Badger said. "There's one below and one above. Stand on the lower spar and hold on to the higher one."

For a moment Ben was unsure what his friend meant, but when he looked he saw that there was a wooden pole projecting out from the mast, with another one above it. The lower one, which looked strong, had sail rolled up beneath it, fastened with loops of rope. He had seen pictures of this sort of thing before and he knew that if the rope were released, the sail would open out below.

Gingerly he made his way out onto the lower spar, gripping the higher one tightly as he did so. He was concentrating so hard on what he was doing that he was almost surprised when Badger appeared beside him.

The other boy beamed at him. "See?" he said. "Easy, isn't it?"

Ben nodded. He would not have described it as easy, but perhaps it was not quite as difficult as he had feared.

"Now we have to check the ropes on this sail," said

Badger. "We have to make sure they're not tangled, so that when somebody pulls on the other end the sail unfurls properly. You watch while I check – that means next time you'll be able to do it by yourself."

Ben held his breath as Badger moved along the spar, reaching down from time to time to rearrange one of the ropes wound around the bunched-up sail. Badger made it all look extremely easy, but all the while Ben was thinking of what would happen if he slipped. It was a long way down to the deck …

It was just as he was thinking this that there came a sudden gust of wind. The air had been quite still up till then, so Ben was caught unawares. As the wind hit the ship, it leaned over and the mast tilted like a giant pencil being moved against the sky. Standing on the spar, Ben felt as if the whole world was shifting under his feet, and his natural reaction was to grab for more support. He should not have done this. He should not have taken his hand off the upper spar, but when your whole world goes topsy-turvy you can easily end up doing the wrong thing.

Ben reached out to grab a rope. As he did so, he lost his footing, and before he knew what was happening he felt himself topple off the spar and into the void. *This is the end*, he thought. *This is the end of me.*

Badger saw what was happening and gave a shout of warning. "Don't let go!" he yelled.

Ben held on to the rope as he fell. For a second or two he plummeted straight down, but then the slack in the rope was taken up and it began to bear his weight. It was an awful wrench to his shoulders, and he felt as if his arms were going to be pulled from their sockets, but he held on to the rope and began to swing.

Out over the deck he swung, and, beyond that, over the sea. Like a giant pendulum he went backwards and forwards, narrowly avoiding the rigging. As he swung inwards, another gust of wind arrived, making the mast swing the other way, so Ben started to swing outwards.

He was aware that Badger was shouting something to him, but he could not make out what it was. There were people on the deck and they were all watching and pointing as he swung about on the end of the rope. He saw Matron appear from below deck, shading her eyes from the sun to get a better view; he saw the Captain; he saw William Edward Hardtack standing with Geoffrey Shark and Maximilian Flubber. Hardtack, Shark and Flubber were looking up and laughing.

Ben's arms were now beginning to ache. He closed his eyes and tried to imagine what it would be like to die. Would it be like having a light switched out? Would it be very painful?

He opened his eyes again. Something was

happening to the rope and he saw that he was getting closer to the deck with each swing. Looking up, he saw that Badger was struggling to loosen the rope, lowering Ben to safety.

Ben did not plan it, but what happened next brought a great roar of approval from many of those watching him from the deck. As the arc of his swing lengthened, he was now close to the deck. On his final swing, he suddenly realised that he was heading straight for Hardtack and his two friends.

"Look out!" Ben shouted. "Get out of the way!"

But it was too late, as he was already upon them. With a great thump he knocked all three of them over like skittles in a bowling alley. Down they went – one, two, three – while Ben, letting go of the rope at last, landed safely on his feet. He almost toppled over, but managed to straighten himself out, astonished to find that he was completely unharmed.

Hardtack was the first of the three to get back on his feet. "You idiot!" he shouted. "You deliberately knocked us down!"

Now Shark and Flubber joined him, rubbing themselves in the places where they had landed. "You stupid —" Shark began.

He did not finish, as the Captain's voice could now be heard booming across the deck. "You there! Hardtack, Shark, Flubber! I saw you laughing at that poor boy. Report to my cabin immediately!"

Ben reached out to grab a rope. As he did so, he lost his footing, and before he knew what was happening he felt himself topple off the spar...

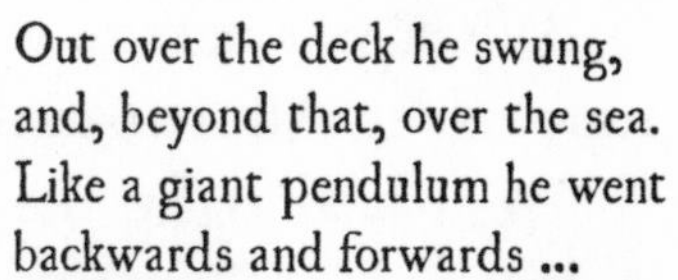

With a great thump he knocked all three of them over like skittles in a bowling alley. Down they went – one, two, three ...

Hardtack shot Ben a furious glance as he led the other two off to the Captain's cabin. Poppy had appeared by now and was standing at Ben's side.

"They're in trouble," she whispered. "And it serves them right."

Ben did not say anything. He did not want to make enemies, but it seemed to him that he now had three people who would be determined to get even.

Badger was next to arrive, having slid down the rope ladder with remarkable speed.

"Are you all right?" he asked.

Ben nodded. "You saved my life," he said to Badger.

"Oh well," said Badger modestly. "Please don't mention it."

Now Matron came over, looking anxious. "That was a narrow escape," she said. "Nothing broken?"

"I'm fine," Ben reassured her.

"You scared me," said Fee to her brother.

"I'm fine," he said again.

Matron left and they stood on the deck, until Poppy said, "Would you like me to show you how to coil rope? You don't have to climb anywhere to do that – we can do that right here on deck."

"That would be a great idea," said Ben, and he followed Poppy to a place on the deck where large bundles of rope were waiting to be wound into neat coils. He felt none the worse for his ordeal, and enjoyed handling the thick rope.

"You're good at this," Poppy complimented him. "I think you're going to be a really good sailor, Ben."

"Thank you," said Ben.

"What was it like swinging on that rope?" asked Poppy. Ben thought for a moment. "Not too bad," he said. But then he added, "Not that I'd like to try it again in a hurry."

The rest of the day seemed to go quickly. Badger showed Ben what to do, making sure that he put himself in no further danger, while Fee followed Poppy around, learning about the tasks she had to perform.

"You're doing just fine," said Poppy. "I was hopeless when I first started. Living out in the bush, I knew all about things like bush tucker and kangaroo tracks, but I hardly knew which end of a boat was which. In fact, I don't think I'd ever *seen* a boat until I came here."

"Bush tucker?" asked Fee.

"It's food you find in the bush," explained Poppy. "There's always something you can eat. You think there's nothing, but then you start scrabbling around – do a bit of digging and so on – and before you know it you've got a three-course meal. Leaves, berries, roots – that sort of thing. The occasional lizard if you're feeling really hungry. Snake too. Ever eaten a snake, Fee?"

Fee made a face. "No thanks!"

"Oh well," said Poppy, with a laugh. "Snake's not for everyone, I suppose."

At six o'clock, a bell sounded and work stopped. "Four bells on the first dog watch," said Badger, putting down the cloth he was using to polish a rail. "That's it."

The first dog watch was the period from four in the afternoon until six in the evening, and a bell was rung after each half hour. Four bells on that watch meant that you could stop whatever you were doing. It was always a welcome signal.

They went down below and changed out of their working clothes. Dinner was an hour later, and before that they could do what they liked. Badger took Ben to introduce him to his friends, and Poppy did the same for Fee. Then, when another bell rang, they all made their way into dinner.

Seated at the table with Badger on his right and a boy called Thomas Seagrape on his left, Ben tucked into the delicious fish stew that Cook had prepared. Thomas was a tall, thin boy from Jamaica. He had a wide smile and a friendly manner, and Ben knew at once that here was another friend. Thomas chatted to him about Port Antonio, where he lived with his mother, a well-known sailor, Captain Sally, who had a small steamer that made the journey between Jamaica and the Cayman Islands once a week. It seemed to Ben that Thomas knew everything there was to know about the sea, but at the same time he was not one of those people who make you feel small because you know only a fraction of what they know.

It was Thomas who brought up the subject of William Edward Hardtack and his gang.

"They're in big trouble," he said, taking a mouthful of fish stew. Thomas continued, but all Ben could hear was an extraordinary spludging, swilling, chomping sound.

"I beg your pardon?" said Ben.

"Sorry," said Thomas, wiping his lips with the back of his hand. "It's difficult to speak when your mouth's full of fish stew. What I was trying to say was that Hardtack and Co. are in serious trouble."

Badger joined in. "Over what happened to Ben?" he asked.

Thomas nodded. "The Captain was furious. I heard him shouting at them. He told them that it had been a dangerous situation and that the last thing you should do in those circumstances is to laugh. He said that in the old days in the navy they would have been whipped with the cat o'nine tails for that sort of thing."

Ben shivered. He had read about the cat o'nine tails, a savage sort of whip, and he did not like the thought of it. Fortunately it had long since been taken out of use, but when it had been used it was truly terrible.

Thomas continued. "Then he gave them their punishment. And you know what it was?"

Ben and Badger both waited, Ben with a sinking feeling in his heart. They would blame him for this – he was sure of it.

"They're on heads-scrubbing duties for a whole week," said Thomas. "A week! Can you imagine it?" He turned to Ben. "You know what the heads are? The toilets. They have to clean the toilets every morning and every evening for a week."

"I'm glad it's not me," said Badger. "I had to do it once. And that was just for one day. It's horrible. You end up all stinky."

Ben said nothing for a while, but then he asked, rather miserably, "Are they here?"

Thomas turned round and scanned the rows of heads at the tables behind them. "It looks like they're still hard at work," he said. "They'll be late for dinner after they've washed up and changed their clothes."

"And that means there'll be hardly any food for them," Badger pointed out. "Cook gets mad if you're late for dinner. He just gives you the scraps. Even Henry gets better food than that."

It was at that moment that William Edward Hardtack, Geoffrey Shark and Maximilian Flubber came into the mess hall. They looked a bit wet – as if they had taken a shower – and every one of them was scowling. Everybody in the mess hall, it seemed, knew what had happened, and smirked and whispered as the three culprits made their way up to the service hatch. Then there was complete silence as the entire school strained to hear what Cook had to say.

He did not disappoint his audience.

"So," said Cook. "Who do we have here, I ask meself? If it isn't William Edward Hardtack and his two faithful side-kicks, Geoffrey Shark, no less, and our charming friend, Maximilian Flubber! Well, well, well! And where have you three young gentlemen been, may I ask?"

Hardtack looked over his shoulder. He did not want to be overheard. "Working, Cook," he mumbled.

"What was that?" snapped Cook. "Speak up, young man."

"Working, Cook," said Hardtack, much louder now.

"Oh?" said Cook. "I thought work stopped at four bells on the first dog watch. Or am I wrong? And what sort of work exactly, my three hearties?"

"Scrubbing the heads," muttered Geoffrey Shark.

Cook gave a crow of delight. "Now there's a good occupation for a fine fellow like yourself, Shark! With your fancy hair-style and all! Well, well! And I take it that you've washed your hands thoroughly? Good. Because you must have clean hands if you're to eat in this expensive restaurant. Not, I hasten to add, that there's much grub left. Sorry about that. Just a few scraps for the three of you."

Cook dispensed a small amount of food to each of the boys and then, with a theatrical gesture, snapped shut the serving hatch. Hardtack and his companions shuffled to their table and sat down amongst their fellow Upper Deckers. At that table nobody dared to giggle or even smile at the public humiliation of the three – William Edward Hardtack was, after all, the Prefect of the Upper Deck – but at all the other tables there was hardly a straight face.

"They really deserve this," said Thomas, gleefully. "I don't like to see people being punished, but sometimes ..."

Badger thought much the same, but Ben stared grimly ahead. He knew that whatever the rights and wrongs of the situation were – and he himself had done nothing on purpose to get those three into trouble – they would blame him for this. If earlier on he had sensed the possibility of making enemies with Hardtack, that possibility was now a certainty.

Badger guessed that this was the way Ben was feeling and tried to reassure him. "Listen, Ben," he said. "Those guys are all hot air. They talk big but they're basically nothing to worry about."

Thomas agreed. "And don't you worry, Ben," he said, laying a comforting hand on Ben's shoulder. "You've got friends. You've got me and Badger here, and a whole lot of other people who can't stand that bunch. I'm telling you, man, there's nothing they can do. Nothing – that's right, isn't it, Badge?"

Badger nodded, but Ben, much as he would have liked to believe what his two new friends said, could tell that they were just trying to cheer him up and that Hardtack, Shark and Flubber were far more than just hot air.

At two bells on the first watch, which on dry land would be nine o'clock at night, the lights in all the sleeping cabins had to be turned out. This was a strict rule, and although most people waited until the last second before obeying it, by one minute past nine every light on the three living decks was extinguished. Since the *Tobermory* was in harbour, none of the students had to be up on deck on watch; that would change once they were at sea, when the night would be divided into three watches that they would take it in turns to stay up for.

"How do you like your hammock?" Badger asked from his side of the cabin. 'You comfortable enough?"

Ben was unsure what to say. It was a strange feeling, he thought – rather like being wrapped in something and then hung up. It was not an uncomfortable sensation, but at the same time it was not really how he would choose to sleep. What if he wanted to stretch out? What if he turned over and found himself either wrapped up tighter and tighter or, worse still, if he fell out onto the floor? He decided to say that he was all right and was sure he would get used to it.

"You will," said Badger. "After a few nights a bed will feel strange to you and you'll want to be back in a hammock."

For a few minutes neither boy said anything. On board a ship there are always all sorts of noises, even at night. There is the creaking of timbers; there is the sound of wind in the rigging; there is the lapping of the waves against the hull. The one thing you never hear on a ship is complete silence.

Then Badger spoke about what had happened on

the mast. "Was today the first time you've ever been in real danger?" he asked.

Ben thought for a few moments before answering. He thought he probably had been, but now that he tried to remember he could not think of any occasion when his life had actually been threatened. So he said yes. Then he asked, "What about you, Badge?"

"Once," said Badger. "It was about a year ago, when I was home during the summer. We get a four-week holiday, you see, in the summer, and I went back to New York. My parents have a house near the ocean up in Maine. We've got a sailing boat – just a small one. It can take two people, but I use it by myself. My parents don't like sailing very much.

"One afternoon I went out in this boat. There wasn't much wind but a few gusts came up and I managed to get get quite far out. Then the wind died away completely."

"So you were stuck?" asked Ben.

"Well, I would have been stuck if it hadn't been for the current. The tide had changed and there was quite a strong current where I was. This was going straight out to sea. It took my boat with it. The shore was getting smaller and smaller and I realised that I was being carried out into the open ocean. There was nothing I could do about it."

"Weren't there any other boats?" asked Ben.

"There were one or two," replied Badger. "But they

were a long way away and they were going in a different direction."

"Couldn't you wave?"

"They were too far away to see me," said Badger.

Ben was silent. Obviously Badger had managed to get out of danger or he would not be able to tell the story now, but it was still a bit frightening.

"Then I remembered something," said Badger. "I had my cell phone with me and I realised that we were not too far off shore for it to work. So I called my dad's phone. It was busy. So I tried my mom's. That was busy too. They were working you see – they do lots of deals from home, even when we're on holiday up there, and they were talking to people in New York.

"I waited for about ten minutes, and then I tried again. The same thing happened. And ten minutes after that, and another ten minutes after that as well. Then my battery gave out."

Ben gasped. "You couldn't call?"

"Not any more," said Badger.

"You were rescued?"

"Yes," said Badger. "But not before I saw a shark. It was a big one and I swear it was circling my boat. The shark was way bigger than the boat and could easily have tipped me over if it had wanted."

"A great white?" asked Ben.

"Probably," said Badger. "They travel a lot and sometimes they get up there."

Ben hardly dared ask what happened next.

"I saw a boat," said Badger. "I was able to take off my shirt and wave it about. They spotted me and came over. They threw me a line. Then I went on board and they towed mine back to shore. They saw the shark too and said how lucky I had been. They said they had heard of someone being tipped out of their boat a few months before and never being seen again. They said they thought it could be the same shark."

"I'm glad you were safe," said Ben.

"So was I," said Badger.

Nothing more was said, apart from "Goodnight", and shortly afterwards, tired from a day of hard work – and danger – Ben found himself drifting off to sleep, lulled by the creaking of timbers and the sound of the wind blowing gently against their porthole. He did not wake up until the following morning when he heard a bell being rung announcing the beginning of the day. It was no ordinary day, of course. This was the day on which the *Tobermory* was to set sail. This was the start of the new school term.

A very narrow escape

The first thing was the muster roll. This took place out in the open, with everybody standing in lines on the main deck and shouting out "*Aye, aye!*" when their names were called. This was done in alphabetical order, starting with Monica Adams and ending with Peter Ziff. When they reached M, and MacTavish B. was called out, followed by MacTavish F., Ben heard a snigger somewhere in a row behind him. He did not turn his head, but he was fairly sure it would be from one of three people, even if he could not see which one it was.

Thomas Seagrape was standing nearby. Lowering his voice, he said to Ben, "Ignore them. That's what I always do."

After the roll call the Captain addressed the whole school. He was wearing his best uniform, with its bright brass buttons, each with a small anchor stamped into the metal. The Captain had a loud voice and everybody was able to hear each word he spoke, even though there were seagulls squawking at the top of their voices above the ship.

"Today we set sail at the beginning of a new term," began the Captain. "You all know what to do, and if you don't, then you'll soon learn. I want you to do your best – that's all. You can't do better than that, can you? No, you can't. And remember this: the sea can be a dangerous place. Have fun, but don't take any risks. Follow commands. Do your work. Stay alert. That's all."

"That's the same speech he gives every term," Poppy whispered to Fee. "We'd all faint with surprise if he said anything new."

Now it was the turn of another teacher to speak. This was Mr Rigger, a man with large arm muscles and the longest moustache ever seen at sea. This moustache was his pride and joy and everybody used it to tell the direction of the wind. If you looked at Mr Rigger's moustache, you could tell whether the wind was in the south-west or the east, or whatever direction it was blowing from. He did not mind people doing this, and if asked he would stand with his head into the wind so that his moustache could be read.

"Mr Rigger teaches seamanship," Poppy explained to Fee. "That's all about how to sail and keep the ship afloat."

Fee's eyes widened. Surely there was no chance of

a ship as big as the *Tobermory* going down. "On our submarine we never had to worry about sinking," she said, "because that's what submarines are meant to do."

Poppy laughed. "Oh, the *Tobermory* is very safe," she assured her friend. "And as for Mr Rigger, he's really nice – he never shouts at you if you get something wrong. And if you get it right, he says

'Lovely-jubberly' and sometimes even gives you a peppermint."

"That's the best sort of teacher," said Fee.

Mr Rigger stepped into the Captain's place.

"Now then, everybody," he began. "We're going to start by getting the ship ready to leave port. You all know your stations." He paused. "Anybody new?'

Hesitantly, Ben and Fee raised their hands.

"Ah yes," said Mr Rigger. "MacTavish F. and MacTavish B. You can start today with the Captain. He'll show you the helm. The rest of you, report to your places in fifteen minutes. Sails, lines, anchor – off you go!"

With fifteen minutes in hand, Ben went over to the railings to look out at Tobermory harbour. Badger and Thomas went with him, and Badger pointed out some of the sights.

"That's the pier over there," he said, pointing to a large stone wall. "You see that caravan parked on it? That sells the best fish and chips in Scotland. You should try them."

"Badge is right," said Thomas. "Badger and I call chips French fries. I dream of them, you know. You should have them next time we're in port, Ben."

"I will," said Ben. He had noticed a large sailing ship riding at anchor not far from the pier. "What's that ship?" he asked.

Badger looked to where Ben was pointing. "Oh,

that," he said. "She's called the *Albatross*. Somebody said that's she's a film ship."

Ben was puzzled. "A film ship?"

"There's a film crew onboard," explained Badger. "They're making a movie about people who go off on a cruise and have all sorts of adventures. Poppy knows something about it. She heard people talking about it on shore."

Ben stared at the ship. Several people in white uniforms – the sailors, he assumed – were using an onboard crane to take on supplies from a small boat.

Badger looked at his watch. "Time's almost up," he said. "You'd better go and report to the Captain." He pointed to where the Captain was standing behind the large wheel near the stern, the ship's back. Fee was already there.

"Good luck," said Badger. "Every new person gets the chance on his first day to help the Captain at the helm. It's a treat to mark the beginning of your sailing career."

Ben made his way to join the Captain and Fee. Once he was there, the Captain explained to the two of them how to steer the ship. He also unfolded a large chart that showed the sea and the surrounding shores.

"The blue bits are the sea," he said. "The green bits are land. The numbers you see on the blue bits are the depth of the sea in that particular place."

Ben and Fee studied the chart. They had seen their parents spread out maps and charts many times before. They noted where Tobermory harbour was and they saw the way out, past a small island, to the Sound of Mull beyond. They saw some rocks marked with a cross and arrows showing the way the currents moved.

"This is where we're going," said the Captain. "There's an island called Canna which is up here." He jabbed at the chart with a finger. "That's where we'll spend the night. We'll anchor in this bay here." He tapped the chart again. "And then the following day, we'll head for this island over here." He indicated land on the chart. The chart was put away in a nearby locker.

"Weigh anchor!" shouted the Captain.

This was the signal for a rumbling, clanking sound to start at the other end of the ship.

"The anchor chain's coming up nicely," said the Captain. After a couple of minutes the last of the chain was wound up and the great anchor, a massive metal hook dripping with mud and seaweed, was cranked into its resting place. Down below could be heard the rumble of the engine and the swishing sound of the propeller. Then, slowly but purposefully, the ship turned her nose into the wind and began to slide through the water.

Ben smiled at Fee, and she smiled back. This was

a big moment for both of them – the beginning of their first voyage on the ship that was to be their school – and their home – for the next few years.

It took them half an hour to work their way up the last of the channel separating the island of Mull from the mainland of Scotland. Then, when they were level with the tip of the island, the wider sea opened up before them. There, far off to the north, was the big Isle of Skye and its smaller islands, scattered in the sea like crumbs thrown into the water. Off to the starboard side were towering cliffs that marked the edge of Scotland. Now it was time to switch off the ship's engine and for the sails to be rolled out. Ben held his breath as he saw people scaling the rope ladders to prepare the sails. He hardly dared look while the great sheets of white canvas flapped and billowed, but then he saw everybody making their way down safely to the deck and he was able to breathe freely again.

As the sails filled, Ben felt the ship leap forward, like a dog let off the leash. At the same time, the deck tilted away from the wind, so that the whole world suddenly seemed to be at a bit of an angle. Fee almost lost her balance, but managed to grab hold of Ben's shoulder and stay upright.

The Captain smiled at her. "It's always a bit odd the first time," he said. "You'll get used to everything being tilted." He paused, and then asked whether she would like to take the helm.

"Me?" said Fee.

"Yes," said the Captain. "You have to learn sooner or later. It's easy enough, and I'll be standing right here beside you."

Ben felt proud of his sister as he saw her take hold of the great wooden wheel and assume control of the ship.

"That's fine," said the Captain. "Keep her on this course now."

The ship was settling down now as the sails were adjusted. Mr Rigger called out orders, telling people to shorten this rope and let that one out. It all seemed rather complicated to Ben and Fee, but everybody seemed to know exactly what to do. The deck was at less of an angle now, and it was possible to walk without feeling as if you were about to topple over.

Badger came by to find out how they were doing. He was impressed to see Fee steering the ship and he told her that he thought she was doing it well. Then he went off to attend to another task, saying that he would see them later on.

As they cleared the top of Mull, they began to meet rather bigger waves. Up to that point, the swell coming in from the Atlantic had broken on the far side of the island – now they felt its full force. This made a difference to the ship, which began to move up and down as it encountered the long, rolling waves.

Ben closed his eyes. He was beginning to feel a strange sensation in the pit of his stomach. It was an odd feeling – not unlike the one you have after eating something that does not agree with you.

The Captain was looking at him. "You all right, MacTavish B?" he asked.

Ben nodded. "I just feel a little bit odd, Captain. Maybe it was one of Cook's sausages ..."

Captain Macbeth smiled. "I don't think you should blame your breakfast," he said. "What you're feeling is as old as sailing itself. Have you never felt seasick before?"

Ben shook his head.

The Captain frowned. "But your parents have that research submarine, don't they? Did you never feel sick on that?"

"It never went up and down," chipped in Fee. "You don't find waves underwater."

"No, I suppose you don't," said the Captain. "So this might be a first for you."

Ben swallowed. He was feeling queasier and queasier now. It was a very unpleasant sensation.

"Listen," said the Captain. "You'd better go and sit down somewhere. Don't go down below – that'll just make it worse. You'll feel better in due course. It never lasts too long."

Ben nodded. He was now feeling so miserable that he had not taken in what the Captain had said. Rather than stay on deck, the thought of lying down in his hammock seemed very appealing. Being careful not to fall over, he made his way across the deck and down the companionway to the deck below. Then he went down a further companionway to reach the middle deck, where his cabin was.

By the time he reached the middle deck, his queasy feelings had become even worse. Now his stomach was in violent revolt, and he realised that before too long he was going to sick. He looked down the passageway towards the signs that said BOYS' HEADS. If he ran quickly, he would probably reach it in time and not be sick in the passageway itself. That would be a disaster for his first day.

He reached the heads more quickly than he imagined. The door was open and in a dreadful moment he saw that there was somebody in there already. And almost immediately he realised who it was: Geoffrey Shark, down on his knees with a bucket and brush, scrubbing the floor. He was carrying out the morning part of his punishment.

Ben was uncertain what to do. Geoffrey Shark was the last person – or one of the last people – he wanted to bump into, and yet at any moment he was going to be sick.

Then Ben became aware that somebody was

coming along the passageway towards him. It was Poppy.

"Are you all right?" she asked.

Ben drew her aside, so they should not be seen by Shark. "I'm going to be sick," he whispered urgently. "But I don't want to go in there while he's ..."

He did not finish. Poppy, understanding the situation, had taken him by the elbow and was propelling him along the passageway towards a sign that said GIRLS' HEADS.

"But I can't go in there," protested Ben. "Boys can't use the girls' bathrooms."

"There's nobody around," said Poppy. "And I'll keep watch for you outside. Go on."

She did not allow him to argue, and pushed Ben through the open door. And she did it just in time, for Ben now felt his stomach heaving up within him. He rushed into the nearest cubicle and stuck his head into the bowl.

It was not pleasant, but he felt much better afterwards, and because he had made it in time there was no mess. But just as he was rinsing out his mouth at one of the basins, he heard voices and the outer door of the heads was slammed shut.

Ben crept towards the closed door. This was every boy's nightmare – to be caught in the girls' heads while a girl waited outside. What would they think of him if he came out? Would they imagine he had just got it wrong, or would they think that he had been up to no good? He felt himself blushing with shame just at the thought of it.

He strained to make out what was being said outside. He recognised Poppy's voice, and then a boy said something in reply.

"I need to get in there to scrub the floor," said Shark. "Open the door."

"No," said Poppy. "A friend of mine is in there. You can't go in there if you're a boy."

"Then tell her to come out," said Shark. "I haven't got all day."

"No," said Poppy. "She's going to be ages. She's washing her hair and brushing her teeth."

"Tell her to hurry up," said Shark. "I'll wait here."

"No you won't," said Poppy. "Boys aren't allowed to wait outside the girls' heads. That's the rule."

"There's no such rule," said Shark. "You're making it up."

"I'm not," said Poppy. "And anyway, here comes Matron. You can ask her."

Geoffrey Shark obviously did not think this was a good idea, as he muttered something and then his steps could be heard going off down the passageway. But now Matron was there, and Ben thought this could make it even worse.

"And what are you doing, Poppy?" asked Matron.

Ben caught his breath as he listened to Poppy's response.

"There's a boy in there, Matron."

Matron's voice sounded disapproving. "There's a boy in the girls' heads?"

"Yes," said Poppy. "It's that new boy, Ben. He was going to be sick and I let him go in there rather than have him being sick all over the passageway. The boys' heads were being cleaned."

"Oh," said Matron. "Well, let's go inside and check if he's all right."

The door was opened and Ben found himself face to face with Matron, and behind her, Poppy.

Matron looked concerned. "Are you all right, Ben?" she asked.

Ben nodded. "I've been seasick, Matron."

"That often happens on the first day," she said. "Come along with me to the sick bay. You can lie down there and I can keep an eye on you."

Ben thanked her, and he thanked Poppy too before he went off with Matron to the sick bay. He was still feeling queasy, but the feeling was not so bad as it had been just a few minutes ago.

"I have some special chewing gum," said Matron. "You can have a piece. It helps with seasickness."

Once in the sick bay, Ben sat down and chewed on the medicinal chewing gum Matron had given him. He felt a great deal better now, and when

Matron came to check up on him an hour later, he felt well enough to go back on deck.

"That's the best thing to do," said Matron. "Fresh air is a great cure for seasickness."

As he left the sick bay, Ben thought about what had happened earlier on. He felt grateful to Poppy for her help, but he found himself wondering what she was doing down on Middle Deck when everybody was meant to be on duty up above. Had she been carrying something? Of course he had had other things on his mind at the time – being just about to be sick – but he thought he remembered that she had had a small bag in her hand. When she had first seen him she had put this behind her back, as if trying to hide it. What was it?

He was still pondering this when he reached the deck. The Captain was at the helm now and there was no sign of Fee.

"Your sister has gone off to do other duties," the Captain said. "Would you like to have a go?"

Ben stood behind the helm, with the Captain at his side. It was an extraordinary feeling having the great ship at his command. A tiny turn on the helm – just the smallest of movements – made the bow swing across the horizon and filled, or emptied, the sails accordingly. It was a sensation of power, but it was also a feeling of being in touch with the world about you – being *part* of the wind, being *part* of the sea.

"You're doing well," said the Captain. "Now just hold that course for a few minutes while I go and check the chart. Don't turn. There are no dangers around. Good deep blue water."

Ben was worried at being left alone at the helm, but he was reassured by the Captain's presence only a few paces away. If anything went wrong, he would be able to be back at the helm within seconds ... not that anything was going to go wrong, of course.

Or so Ben thought. Now he was about to learn one of the lessons that the sea is only too ready to teach – that unexpected things can happen quickly, and when you are least expecting them.

Ben was paying attention. The Captain had told him to look out for other ships, and he was doing just this when he saw a dark patch in the water ahead. At first he thought he was imagining it – when you stare at the sea for a long time the eyes can play tricks on you. Waves can seem bigger than they are. The wind on the face of the water can look like the effect of a current below the surface. There are so many ways in which you can be tricked into seeing things that are not really there. But this dark patch did not go away – nor did it move. There it was in the water, and it was directly ahead of them.

Ben strained his eyes to make out what it was. The Captain had said there was deep water in every direction. And yet he was now as sure as he possibly could be that there was something ahead of them, and that if the ship did not swerve quickly they would hit whatever it was.

He hesitated for a few seconds, and then made up his mind. Swinging the ship's wheel sharply, he felt the shudder of the deck beneath him as the great ship's sails reacted to the turn. He heard the surprised shouts of the crew. Now the wind was blowing directly on the side of the ship, and the canvas strained and creaked as it felt the increased pressure. For the sails and the masts, it was as if a giant invisible hand had suddenly pressed against them.

The Captain gave a shout, returned to the helm, and snatched the wheel from Ben. He began to turn the ship back on its original course.

"There was a rock," shouted Ben. "Look, there it is, Captain."

The Captain peered off to where Ben was pointing. "My goodness!" he exclaimed. "That shouldn't be there. That rock is definitely not on the charts."

Now they were joined by Mr Rigger. He had run across the deck to find out what was happening, his moustache catching the wind and twirling like a weather-vane.

"Look over there, Mr Rigger," said the Captain. "A rock, if I'm not mistaken."

Mr Rigger followed the Captain's gaze. "No, you're

not mistaken, Captain," he said. "And that was a neat bit of helming, if I may say so. Your turning so sharply saved the day, I think."

The Captain smiled, and nodded towards Ben. "Not me, Mr Rigger. It was this young man's doing. He saw it and took evasive action."

Mr Rigger looked at Ben with admiration. "Did he now?" he said. "That was one amazing piece of sailing, if you ask me. Lovely-jubberly, in fact. I think you'll be doing well in my sailing classes."

Ben had been looking down at his shoes as Mr Rigger spoke. He was a modest boy and did not like to be singled out for praise. Some people love that – nothing suits them more than to be the centre of attention – but Ben had never been like that.

If you look down at your shoes, though, you can miss what is going on about you. And so Ben had not seen the small crowd that had gathered to find out what had happened. This included Fee and Poppy, Thomas Seagrape, a girl called Angela Singh, and … Maximilian Flubber. Ben and Fee had only met Angela briefly, but they already liked her. She had rather large front teeth, but these just made her smile all the warmer – when it came. She was shy, though, and a little bit nervous, thought Fee, although both Ben and his sister had decided that she would be a good friend.

Standing next to Angela, Flubber was listening

"You're doing well," said the Captain. "Now just hold that course while I go and check the compass. Don't turn. There are no dangers around. Good deep blue water ..."
SCHOOL SHIP TOBERMORY
... he was now as sure as he possibly could be that there was something ahead of them, and that if the ship did not swerve quickly they would hit whatever it was ...
" ... that was one amazing piece of sailing, if you ask me. Lovely-jubberly, in fact. I think you'll be doing well in my sailing classes!"

intently, his expression seemingly one of innocent interest.

"All right, everybody," said the Captain. "The danger has passed – thanks to this attentive young man." He pointed to Ben and gave a broad smile. "Well done, Ben. You've saved the ship from a nasty encounter with an unpleasant-looking rock. And on your first day too! Extra ice cream for you tonight."

This brought a cheer from Poppy. "Good on you, Ben!" she shouted.

"Yes, well done!" echoed Maximilian Flubber. Ben was surprised to be congratulated by Flubber and looked discreetly at the other boy's ears. He remembered that Flubber's ears were said to move when he told a lie or said something he did not mean, and now Ben was sure that he saw movement.

The Captain turned to Mr Rigger. "Would you have a word with Cook, Mr Rigger? Tell him there's to be extra ice cream for MacTavish B. at dinner tonight."

"Aye, aye, sir," said Mr Rigger.

Ben was now told to go off and help Badger, who was in charge of one of the lower sails. "You've done enough helming for one day," said the Captain. "It's time for you to learn a little about the sails. Badger will show you."

When Ben found Badger, his friend had already heard about what had happened. "It's all round the

ship," said Badger. "Everybody knows about it now. You're the hero of the day, Ben."

Ben tried to play it all down. "I just swung the wheel," he said. "It wasn't anything special."

"It's knowing when to swing the wheel that's the important thing," said Badger. "And you did know."

Ben shrugged. "I'm not sure …"

Badger put a finger to his lips in a sign of silence. "Someone's coming," he said.

It was William Edward Hardtack.

"Max Flubber's given me some interesting news," Hardtack said with a sneer. "So who's the big hero?

Who saved the ship from a rock, I wonder? Well, if it wasn't Ben MacTavish – the great sailor and spotter of rocks. Well done, Mr MacTavish! The Captain's pleased, I hear."

Ben said nothing.

"So what do you think, Badger?" asked Hardtack. "Do you think it was a real rock?" He did not wait for the answer, but continued, "Because you know what? I don't think it was."

"We don't want to hear what you think, Hardtack," retorted Badger. "We're busy."

"You don't want to hear what I've got to say?" sneered Hardtack. "Well, that's tough, because I'm going to tell you anyway. That rock – that so-called rock – was just a big clump of floating seaweed. That's what it was. I saw it myself. I thought: *Is that a rock or is it floating seaweed?* And when I looked again I knew. It was seaweed – no doubt about it. So you turned the ship to avoid a piece of harmless seaweed! That's not so smart, is it?"

"It was a rock," said Badger. "I saw the waves breaking over it. Waves don't break over clumps of seaweed."

William Edward Hardtack ignored this. "I suppose you're really pleased with yourself," he hissed. "Well, we'll see about that!"

And with that he moved away in the slouching, sideways motion that unpleasant people often use.

"Pay no attention to him," said Badger. He searched for the words to express his feelings. "He's just a … he's just a jellyfish!"

They both laughed at the ridiculous description. But it made Ben feel a little better, as laughing at a bully can often help.

Badger looked at Ben, and smiled. "It was definitely a rock, you know," he said. "And what you did was terrific. You're going to be a great sailor, Ben."

Ben thanked him. He was glad that he had such a good friend in Badger, who made him feel much better about being new and not really knowing what to do. He hoped that one day he would be able to repay him for his kindness. He had no idea how he would do this, but he hoped for the chance anyway.

Poppy and Fee share a secret

By late afternoon that day they were close to Canna, the island where they were to spend the night at anchor, tucked away in a snug bay. There they would be protected from the wind and waves and they had been told they would even be able to go ashore. Although small, and with hardly anybody living on it, Canna had a shop that also served tea and cold drinks and was a popular place for visitors. The shop sold postcards. There were plenty of people on the *Tobermory* who were keen to send a postcard home.

That included Badger.

"I'm not sure if there's much point," he said to Ben, "but I like to do it anyway."

Ben stared at his friend in astonishment. "You mean your parents don't read them?"

Badger shrugged. "Sometimes – maybe. I don't know. They never reply."

Ben was unsure what to say. Not having really been away from home before, he had never had to send his parents a postcard. But of course they went away rather often on their research submarine, leaving Ben and Fee with their aunt, and they always wrote from the ports they visited, and telephoned too, or called on their special underwater radio.

He wanted to comfort Badger. "I'm sure they read them," he said. "Or would like to – if they had the time. You told me they're busy."

"Yes, they are," said Badger. "They work all the time. They make a lot of money." He shrugged. "That's what they do, I suppose."

But there was no time to think about parents and postcards as the *Tobermory* sailed gently into the bay. Mr Rigger said that Ben should stick with Badger and Fee should stay with Poppy. "Watch what they do so that you can do it next time," he said. "That's the way we learn at sea."

Poppy and Fee reported for anchor duty. Their job was to watch the anchor chain as it played out of the bow – the nose of the ship – with a loud clanking sound. As the heavy links disappeared into the water, they had to call out if the ship showed any sign of riding over the chain or if the chain itself went off in the wrong direction. They used hand signals to send messages back to the person at the helm. An arm stretched out to the left meant go to port; an arm out to the right meant turn to starboard. And a moving backwards and forwards of the arm, with the palm of the hand flat, meant stop.

"It's simple," said Poppy cheerfully. "Anybody can do it."

Fee was not so sure. She had watched Poppy for much of the day and had been impressed by the other girl's ability to do everything as if it were the easiest task in the world. Fee thought that she would never remember even half of what Poppy knew. She was already dreading the moment when she had to do something for herself, unable to turn to Poppy and ask her how to do it.

Once the anchor was firmly lodged on the seabed, the ship's engine was turned off. Now the Captain gave a signal to everybody on deck that they were off duty and could do what they liked. One of the liberty boats – the small boats used to ferry people ashore – would soon be winched down and be ready to take people onto the island. Since just about everybody was keen to see what the island was like, the boat would have to make several trips to get them all to the pier.

"You'll be collected in time for dinner," the Captain announced. "So make sure you're ready at the pier in exactly one hour."

As they made their way to the island, another sailing ship arrived to drop anchor in the bay. Fee recognised it immediately. "That's the boat we saw in Tobermory," she said, pointing. "That's the *Albatross*."

Poppy and Badger looked round.

"Why yes," said Badger. "That's the one with the film crew."

"Maybe we'll get a part in their movie," said Poppy.

Henry, the Captain's dog, was with them in the liberty boat, although the Captain himself was staying on board. When Henry saw the other ship, he started to bark loudly. He did not seem to be pleased.

"He thinks this bay is his yard," said Badger. "Dogs don't like other boats coming into their yard." Poppy reached out to pat Henry. This calmed him down, although he continued to growl at the *Albatross*.

"Perhaps Henry would like a part in their movie too," suggested Badger. "He could be an extra."

"An extra?" asked Ben. "What's that?"

Badger explained. Extras, he said, were people you saw in the background of movies. They were the people walking around or driving cars or doing any of the ordinary things that people did. They made the whole thing look real.

"I was an extra once," said Badger, just a little proudly. "I had to ride my bike along a street and throw a newspaper onto somebody's porch. I didn't have to say anything. I just rode my bike."

Ben was impressed. It seemed to him that Badger had seen much more of the world than he had and knew far more about it.

"Did you get paid?" asked Poppy.

"I did," said Badger. "But I had to do it seven times, because one of the main actors kept getting it wrong. They had to do the scene over and over again." He remembered something else. "One of the other extras got into a bit of trouble. He had to pretend to be asleep – that was all he had to do. But he kept sneezing, and they said that wasn't what they wanted. They said that you don't sneeze when you're asleep."

"Don't you?" asked Fee. "Are you sure?"

"Of course you don't," said Badger. "If you sneeze when you're asleep, you wake yourself up."

The discussion was cut short by the liberty boat's arrival at the pier. Everybody disembarked, and the boat returned to the *Tobermory* to collect the next group of people. Those who had come ashore made their way to the small local store, ready to spend the pocket money they had brought with them. As Badger had predicted, there were plenty of postcards and stamps for sale, as well as chocolates and other tempting treats.

It was while they were still in the store that a small group arrived from the *Albatross*. There was a tall man with his hair tied back in a pony tail, a woman with a two-way radio in her pocket, and a young man of about eighteen who was carrying a camera with a large lens. As they entered the shop, these three looked about them with an inquisitive air. Seeing Badger, the young man whispered something to the man with the pony tail. The man stared at Badger for a few moments before going over to speak to him.

"You people from that training ship?" he asked.

Badger replied that they were. He explained that the *Tobermory* was a school ship, and that they were at the beginning of a new term.

"Great," said the man. "And can you tell me the name of your Captain?"

"He's called Captain Macbeth," he said. "But everybody just calls him Captain."

The man smiled. "Captain Macbeth is a great name," he said. "I'll take a boat over to see him."

The three visitors then went out of the shop, leaving Badger and his friends to look at one another in puzzlement.

"What on earth was that about?" asked Poppy.

Badger shrugged. "Maybe he wants some help?" he said. "They don't look as if they know much about sailing."

At their feet, Henry gave a low growl.

"Something's bugging Henry," said Fee.

"He didn't like them," said Poppy. "I could tell from the way that he was looking at them. He was suspicious."

"Suspicious of what?" asked Ben.

Poppy had no answer. But she did have something to say about dogs and their ways. "We had a dog at our place in the outback," she said. "There was one of the men who came to do sheep shearing that he just didn't like. He always growled at him and tried to bite him. It was really embarrassing. But then we found out why."

"Had he hurt him?" asked Badger. "Dogs remember people who are cruel to them."

Poppy shook her head. "No, he'd done nothing to him. But the sheep shearer was a thief. He was wanted by the police in South Australia for stealing cattle. It was as if the dog knew."

"Maybe he saw his face on a wanted poster," said Badger, grinning.

"You may laugh, Badger," said Poppy. "But I'm telling you – dogs know when someone's bad. They just know."

They returned to the ship just in time for dinner. Then, while they were all seated in the mess hall, the Captain came in to speak to them. He and the other teachers normally had their meals in a separate room, but whenever he had to make an announcement the Captain came into the mess hall.

"Now listen to me," began the Captain.

This brought complete quiet. When the Captain said 'Now listen to me' it was the signal for all noise to stop.

"I have had a visit from the owner of that ship that some of you will have already seen – the one anchored over there." He pointed out of a porthole. "He's a well-known film director and is making a movie in these waters about a group of people who are kidnapped by pirates."

For a brief moment there was a hum of excited chatter – then silence once more.

"He had a request," the Captain went on. "They need a number of extras. They've been let down by an agency and they need people to play various non-speaking roles – apprentice pirates and so on."

This brought a gasp from just about everyone.

"Now then," said the Captain, "I gave the matter some thought. I know that term has just begun and that you all have a lot of work to do …"

From here and there came groans. It was just their luck, thought some, that schoolwork would spoil a chance like this.

"But," continued the Captain, "I'm aware that proper classes haven't started just yet, and a couple of days won't make much difference to how much you learn."

This resulted in cheering – and the throwing into the air of caps and other nautical headgear – most of which were caught again, although some ended up on the deck.

The Captain held up a hand to restore order. "There are twenty places, and since I imagine that every single one of you would like to take part, we're going to have to draw lots to make it fair. Mr Rigger will write everybody's name on a slip of paper and then we'll get Matron to pick out twenty names from a hat. The lucky twenty will have two days of filming out at sea. They'll spend the day on the *Albatross* and then come back to the *Tobermory* to spend the night. That's all."

This news brought a wave of excited chatter.

"I hope I'm chosen," Fee said to Poppy.

"Me too," said Poppy. "But we probably won't be. It'll be people like Hardtack and Shark – you just see."

"You never know," said Fee.

There was only one topic of conversation during their meal that evening – the possibility of becoming an extra. There were one or two people who pretended not to care whether or not they were chosen, but nobody asked for their name to be taken out of the draw. William Edward Hardtack was especially scornful of the whole idea. "Who wants be in a movie?" he asked sneeringly at the Upper Deck mess table.

Maximilian Flubber was about to say, "*Me – I do*," but bit his tongue when he realised that this was not the answer Hardtack wanted to hear. So instead he muttered, "Not me. Never." And Geoffrey Shark, who probably wanted to be in a movie more than anything else in the world – he was such a vain boy

– made a sound that was meant to be dismissive of the whole idea but that came out, instead, like the sound the plug-hole of a bath tub makes when the last of the bathwater disappears. "I would never settle for being an extra," said Shark. "Waste of time. Complete waste of time."

At the Middle Deck table everyone felt that being an extra could lead to much greater things. "A lot of famous film stars started out as extras," said Poppy.

Badger looked doubtful. "Well, I was an extra," he pointed out, "and yet I'm not a movie star."

"Just have patience," said Poppy. "People wait a long time for the call to come, and they're just about to give up when the phone rings and it's Hollywood."

"I've waited for ages," said Badger, with a grin. "Ages and ages. In fact, I've been waiting for so long I've forgotten that I'm waiting."

But of course they would all have to wait, as Mr Rigger had come in halfway through the meal to tell them that the draw would take place first thing the next morning. "You'll find out then," he said. "It will be absolutely fair. The names are to be put into Cook's white hat and will be picked out by Matron, who will have her eyes closed."

"Very fair hat, my hat is!" shouted Cook. "Anybody disagree?"

Nobody spoke. You did not argue with Cook – not if you wanted any breakfast.

As he climbed into his hammock that night, Ben thought back over his first full day of sailing. Time had passed quickly – probably because everything had been so new and unexpected. It seemed to him that there was a lot to remember, and he wondered whether he would ever master everything he had to learn. It was easy to look as if you knew what you were about, but that did not mean that you really did know. A lot of people were like that, thought Ben, and if you asked them why they were doing what they were doing they would not be able to give you much of an answer.

He was getting used to the hammock, just as Badger had said he would. Although the bay in which they were anchored was sheltered, there was still a bit of movement in the ship. This came from small waves that found their way around the headland. They made a rocking movement, and this in turn made the hammocks swing slightly. It was just the right motion to lull him off to sleep.

Ben found himself drifting. Now he was halfway between being awake and being asleep. He was thinking of the rock he had spotted. What would have happened if he had failed to see it? What would have happened if he had not swung the wheel and sent the ship off on a different course? Rocks were a danger for submarines too, and he had often heard his father warn about them. "The one thing you have to remember," he had said, "is that rocks don't move. Boats move. Waves move. But rocks, as a general rule, don't move. So when you hit a rock, it makes a great big hole in whatever hits it."

If they had hit that rock, the *Tobermory* could well have sunk. Ben imagined what that would have been like. Water would have poured in, and although they had pumps, these might not have been able to cope. The ship would have floundered – like a drowning creature in the water, sinking lower and lower beneath the waves until only the masts could be seen. And then those would go too, and all that would be left would be bits and pieces of equipment – boxes, ropes, deck shoes – floating on the surface. And there would be people in the water too, bobbing around in their lifejackets, waiting to be rescued. Ben was tired, but he was not too tired to give a shudder at the thought. The ship had life rafts – he had seen them – but would there be enough room for everyone? And what if you ended up in a life raft with somebody like Hardtack?

He tried to get these thoughts out of his mind, and was deliberately thinking of something more pleasant, when he heard footsteps outside. Then came the sound of somebody coughing, followed by the low murmur of voices. He was puzzled. The rules were clear: once lights were out there was to be no wandering around. You stayed in your cabin until it was time to get up in the morning, and you were only allowed to go out if you needed to go to the bathroom. *Not bathroom*, he thought: *heads*.

Ben's curiosity got the better of him. Slipping out of his hammock, he made his way across the cabin to the door. Badger was fast asleep by now, wrapped up tightly in his hammock, his eyes firmly closed.

Ben stopped at the door and listened. He heard nothing now but the creaking of timbers. There were no voices. But then he froze: the door handle was slowly beginning to turn. Somebody on the other side was trying to open it.

It was a frightening moment for Ben, and he had no idea what to do. But then he heard a voice on the other side – a girl's voice. "No, not that door," the voice said. "It's further down."

The door handle stopped moving. There were footsteps, and then silence. Ben took a deep breath, summoned up all his courage, and cautiously began to open the door. Then, poking his head outside, he looked down the passageway.

There were no lights on in the passageway but Ben was able to make out, at the far end, two figures just about to disappear through a doorway. He could not see their faces, of course, but one of them seemed taller than the other, and they both looked familiar. Yes, it must be Poppy. There was just something about the way she walked that seemed familiar. *Yes*, he said to himself. *Yes, it's her.*

Once the two figures had disappeared, Ben went out into the passageway and made his way down to the end. He tried to make no noise, and when he reached the door through which they had vanished, he even held his breath. He listened – there were voices, or rather, there were whispers. He strained to hear what was being said, but the closed door made it difficult.

Suddenly he heard a voice he recognised. Even if it was whispering, the voice was one that he would know anywhere – it was Fee's.

"I think we should go back," she said. "You'll be all right, won't you?"

Another, much quieter voice, could be heard. "Come on ..." said that voice. And he knew at once this was Poppy.

Realising that Poppy and Fee might come out at any moment, Ben made his way back to his cabin as quickly as he could. Closing the door behind him, he spun round as he heard a voice behind him.

Badger had woken up and was staring at Ben from his hammock. "Where have you been?" he asked in an accusing tone.

Ben explained. "I heard somebody in the passageway. I went to see who it was."

"And?" prompted Badger.

"It was Poppy and Fee."

Badger sounded puzzled.

"What were they doing?"

Ben shrugged. "I don't know. I heard them talking about something, but I don't know what it was."

"I'm pretty sure Poppy's hiding something," said Badger. "She looked preoccupied the other day – as if her mind was on something else altogether – but she wouldn't tell me what it was."

Ben told him about how he had met Poppy down below when he had been feeling seasick. "She was carrying something in a bag," he said. "I didn't see what it was."

"Very strange," said Badger. He paused before continuing. "Will you ask Fee?"

"I could," said Ben. He and his sister had no secrets from one another – or so he had always believed. Perhaps it would be different now, but at least he could ask.

Badger sounded pleased. "Good," he said. "If I hear about a secret, I always like to know what it is."

Ben thought about this as he climbed back into his hammock. He was feeling tired now and it would not be long before he drifted off to sleep. As he closed his eyes and said goodnight to Badger, he thought of all the possible things that Fee and Poppy might be hiding. Did they have some sort of secret society – a club that only they and a few others would know about? If so, what would it be called, and what

Ben told Badger how he had met Poppy down below when he had been feeling seasick. "She was carrying something in a bag," he said. "I didn't see what it was."

would it be for? Would boys be allowed to join?

Or was it something altogether different – something he had absolutely no idea about; something perhaps just a little bit mysterious?

I'm going to find out, he said to himself, as sleep overtook him.

The names in Cook's hat

The draw took place after breakfast the next morning.

"Now pay attention, everybody," shouted Mr Rigger, as the whole school stood lined up on the deck. "I've prepared a slip of paper for each name."

He gestured to a pile of pieces of paper before him.

"Now," continued Mr Rigger, "I'm going to ask Cook to remove his hat. I shall place all the slips in the hat and invite Matron to pick out twenty. Do you understand me so far?"

Ben was about to shout "*Yes!*" but he heard everybody shouting "*Aye, Aye!*" And so that's what he shouted too. "Good," continued Mr Rigger. "Here we go."

Once the slips of paper were tipped into his upturned chef's hat, Cook held it out in front of himself. Then Matron stepped forward and dipped her hand into the hat. As she did so, she closed her eyes so she could not see the slip she was picking.

"Right," said Mr Rigger, taking the first slip from Matron. "Who have we here?"

The whole school held its breath.

"The first name," announced Mr Rigger, "is … Angela Singh."

A cheer arose from the Lower Deck lines. Angela Singh was a popular member of her deck, and she was liked too by the other decks.

"Well done, Angela," said Matron as she fished into the hat for the second name. "Now then, who's next?"

The next name was read out – a boy from the Upper Deck – and then the next and the one after that. Then it was time for the fifth name.

"William Edward Hardtack," said Mr Rigger.

For a moment there was silence, and then came a few half-hearted cheers from the Upper Deck. Hardtack punched the air in triumph. "Yes!" he shouted. "Yes!"

"Now," said Mr Rigger, taking a slip from Matron, "here we have … Thomas Seagrape."

Ben caught Thomas's eye and smiled. "Well done," he said.

"And now," said Mr Rigger, "the next one is … Geoffrey Shark."

"That's two of them!" groaned Badger. "Hardtack *and* Shark."

William Edward Hardtack gave a whoop of

delight, punching the air again in triumph, just as he had done when he himself had been chosen.

The draw continued. Neither Ben nor Fee was chosen, nor were Poppy and Badger.

"I don't care," said Poppy. "I would have liked it, but I don't care now that Hardtack and Shark are going to be there."

"They'll spoil it for everybody," said Badger.

"Yes," said Poppy. "That's one movie I won't be watching."

They had begun to turn away when suddenly they heard Mr Rigger clapping his hands.

"Hold on, everyone," he said. "Matron has pointed out a problem."

They stayed where they were, curious to find out what this problem could be.

"I'm told," Mr Rigger continued, "that Bartholomew Fitzhardy – whose name I pulled out of the hat – is in fact in the sick bay – and will have to stay there for the next week or so. It's a case of ..." He looked to Matron for guidance.

"Infectious boils," said Matron cheerfully. "Infectious boils with complications."

"It's a case of infectious boils," Mr Rigger continued. "And that means we have only nineteen names. I shall have to draw one final name out of the hat."

This announcement caused considerable excitement. Suddenly there was a chance again, and everybody thought it possible – just possible – that his or her name would be called out.

Matron reached into Cook's hat and extracted a name. "Now then," he said, looking out over the assembled crew, "I have a name here and that name is ..."

Fee closed her eyes. *If I don't look*, she said to herself, *then it will be me.*

Poppy took a deep breath and looked up at the sky. *If I promise to be really good*, she said to herself, *then my name will be called out, even if it means putting up with Hardtack and Shark ...* And she promised to be really good, straight away, with no conditions.

Mr Rigger was ready to announce the name. "The name I have is ... MacTavish B."

Ben gasped. "Me?" he said.

"You're the only MacTavish B. on board," said Badger. "Well done, Ben."

In his excitement at being chosen, Ben did not see Hardtack call Flubber and Shark to his side and whisper something to them. He did not see Shark turn to look in his direction and grin. He did not see Flubber looking over too, smiling. He saw none of that, but Badger did, and Badger swallowed hard. His friend was going to be in the company of Hardtack and his gang for several days and he – Badger – would not be there to defend him. He would have to have a quiet word with Thomas Seagrape and warn him of the danger that he thought Ben might face. Then at least there would be somebody who would be able to look out for Ben when Hardtack made his move, whatever that move might be, and whenever he might make it.

Ben did not have long to pack his kitbag, but he did not have much to put in it. He needed his lifejacket, of course, and a change of clothing in case he got wet. He was also able to pack some chocolate that he still had from the supply his mother had given him before he joined the *Tobermory*. With these things all tucked into the kitbag, Ben was ready to say goodbye to Fee, Badger and the others who would be staying behind.

He had one thing still to do, and this involved Fee. He had not forgotten what he had seen the previous night, and he remembered, too, what he had said to Badger about it. He was going to ask her – as directly as necessary – what she and Poppy were up to.

The opportunity soon arose, as Fee came over to wish him good luck on the other ship.

"You'll have an interesting time," she said. "You're lucky."

Ben thanked her, and said that he wished that she had been chosen too. Then he asked her, "What are you and Poppy up to, Fee?"

His question had an instant effect. Blushing

deeply, Fee stared at her brother. "I don't know what you mean," she answered.

Ben frowned. "You do, Fee. You do know what I mean." She shook her head vigorously. "No, I don't."

Ben leaned towards his sister so that he was looking directly into her eyes. "Listen, Fee," he said pointing his finger at her. " I saw you! I saw you and Poppy last night in the passageway. I saw you going into that cabin at the end. You were talking to somebody."

Fee looked away, uncertain what to do.

"So," said Ben. "So you should tell me, Fee. You've never hidden things from me before."

It was clear to him that his sister was struggling. One part of her, he thought, wanted to tell him everything, but there was another part that was saying, *Hold on!*

He decided to try a different tack. "Are you scared to tell me?"

She looked at him and opened her mouth to speak. "It's not that ..."

Fee stopped. Poppy had joined them and was looking at her anxiously. "What are you talking about?" the Australian girl asked.

"Nothing," said Fee.

Poppy glanced at Ben. "Are you sure?" she said.

Ben was unsure what to do. He could see that his sister was unwilling to talk, and he could see, too, that of the two girls, Poppy was a bit older, and a bit bigger, and was obviously in charge. If he pressed the matter now, he could make things awkward for Fee. He had instantly liked Poppy, but was she a good influence on his sister? He wasn't sure now. Ben decided to hope for the best. "I'd better go," he said. "We'll be going across to the *Albatross* in a couple of minutes."

"Good luck," said Poppy. "Have fun."

Fee, who was clearly relieved, went forward to give her brother a goodbye hug. As she did so, she whispered into his ear, "I'll tell you – I promise you. But not just yet."

They needed two boats to take all twenty people over to the *Albatross*. Then, when the ferrying was done, both ships hauled up their anchors and began to sail out of the bay. For safety reasons they kept some distance from each other – ships need lots of room when they are at sea – and this made it hard for those on the *Tobermory* to see exactly what was happening on the *Albatross*. They could see, though, that there were large piles of equipment on deck, and people were milling about these.

On board the *Tobermory*, ordinary activities continued. Now that they had embarked on their voyage, the normal school routine could begin. This meant that Fee and Poppy found themselves sitting next to one another in a classroom as a geography lesson began. As they were on a school ship, geography was mostly about the sea rather than the land. There were the names of all the oceans and the seas to learn; there were maps of currents to be studied; and there was a great deal of information on how great rivers run into the sea and where they do this. Fee found this all fascinating, and copied out the names of the oceans carefully on the first page of her notebook: *Atlantic Ocean, Pacific Ocean, Indian Ocean*, she wrote. There were two more, to make five: *Arctic* and *Southern.* Then she wrote: *The biggest is the Pacific Ocean and the smallest is the Arctic Ocean.*

The teacher who taught them about oceans was called Miss Worsfold. She was a small woman whom Fee had seen on deck but had never met. She was small indeed – smaller than most of the students – but she made up for her lack of size with sheer energy, and with the brightness of her eyes. These were of a deep blue colour – "rather like an ocean," Poppy had said – and they flashed with light. Poppy had told Fee that she would like her, and Fee found that this was so. There was something about Miss Worsfold that made you believe she understood what you felt.

"Not only are there oceans," said Miss Worsfold, "but there are seas too."

Poppy put up her hand. "The Caribbean Sea," she said.

"Exactly," said Miss Worsfold.

Fee joined in. "The Mediterranean Sea, Miss Worsfold," she said.

"Well done," said Miss Worsfold.

The geography lesson went on for some time. Next were two hours during which the sails were taken in and the ship simply bobbed up and down on the sea, going nowhere. This was because the *Albatross* had stopped to do some filming, and the two ships were to stay within sight of each other.

"If anybody wants to swim," said Mr Rigger, "then you may do so – as long as you stay close to the ship."

It was a warm day, and this suggestion was popular. Poppy, though, had a better idea. "Did Matron say anything to you about diving lessons?" she asked Fee.

Fee nodded. "When we saw her photograph, we asked and she said that she would teach us."

"Good," said Poppy. "She promised me too. Let's find her." The two girls went off to Matron's cabin and knocked on the door. Matron was in, and asked them what they wanted.

Fee felt a bit shy, but asked nonetheless. "Could you teach us how to dive?"

"Of course I will," said Matron. "What a good idea, MacTavish F!"

Once changed into their swimming costumes, the two girls joined Matron on deck. Matron was wearing an elegant silver swimsuit and a tight-fitting swimming cap that had the Olympic ring symbol on its front. "Now then," she said, "I shall begin by demonstrating a dive. Then I'll show you the basic techniques. Watch closely, girls."

Fee and Poppy watched as Matron began to climb up one of the rope ladders that led up towards the top of the mast.

Fee was nervous. "Is she going to go right up to the top?" she asked.

"No," said Poppy. "She won't go that far."

Poppy was right, Matron stopped about halfway up. There she turned, and holding onto the rope ladder with one hand, she stretched the other one out in front of her. Then, for a breath-taking moment, she balanced on the rope beneath her feet before letting go and launching herself out into the void below.

Fee gave an involuntary gasp. She was worried that Matron would hit the side of the ship on her way down, but that did not happen. As perfectly as an arrow shot from a bow, Matron cut through the air. Then, with what seemed like no splash at all, she entered the sea, cutting into the surface with all the cleanness of a knife. For a few moments she was lost to view, but then she popped up, waved and swam back to the side of the ship.

Back on deck, she smiled at the two girls. "You see," she said. "It's easy."

Poppy looked up at the rope ladder. "Do we have to go up there?" she asked.

Matron laughed. "Of course not. You can dive from the side of the ship – it's much easier that way."

She led the girls to the side, and talked them through the proper way to dive. There was rather a lot to remember, thought Fee: you had to keep your arms together, make sure that your legs did not flip over backwards, and not land on your stomach.

"It's not as hard as it sounds," said Matron. "Now you go first, Poppy."

Poppy stood on the side of the ship, stretched out her arms, and dived. She entered the water at the wrong angle, but Matron seemed pleased enough. It was not a perfect dive, but a strong start. Then it was Fee's turn.

Standing at the side of the ship, looking down into the sea below, Fee wondered why she had asked for diving lessons in the first place. There were plenty of easier ways of entering the water, she thought. Jumping was one of them, and that was how she had always done it before, even when she had intended to dive. Or climbing down a ladder and lowering yourself in bit by bit. But that was not the point: this was a diving lesson and they were waiting for her to try.

She almost jumped, but then, in her mind's eye, she saw Matron, and she thought: *I'm going to do this for her!* It worked. Taking a deep breath, she closed her eyes, and fell forward into the air. Down she went, so quickly, she thought. And then there was a rush of water and the sudden shock of the cold. And green all about her. And bubbles. And the taste of salt.

Before she knew it, she was back on the surface. Above her, looking over the edge of the ship, were Matron and Poppy.

"Excellent!" shouted Matron. "A first-class dive, Fee!"

Fee could hardly believe she'd done it. She couldn't wait to tell Ben. She would also write and tell her parents. Diving felt just like going under water in a submarine. They would be interested to hear that, she thought.

The extras came back in the early evening, just as dinner was being served. Ben and Thomas Seagrape joined their friends at the Middle Deck table and immediately faced a barrage of questions. What was it like on the *Albatross*? Did he speak to the director? What costumes did they wear? It seemed that everybody wanted to know even the smallest detail of what had happened.

Thomas started by explaining the roles they had to play. "We are meant to be the crew of a ship that has been taken over by pirates," he said. "So we were all dressed in nineteenth-century sailors' clothes –

you know, britches and those shirts you don't tuck in. They weren't comfortable."

"No," said Ben. "Mine scratched badly and I still feel a bit itchy."

Thomas glanced at Ben. "Should I tell them?" he asked.

"Tell us what?" said Poppy.

Ben nodded. "You may as well. They'll hear soon enough, anyway."

Thomas sighed. "There were two main parts available," he said. "So they said that two of the extras would be chosen for these."

"Starring parts?" enquired Poppy, her eyes wide. "Why would a film company give these roles to the likes of us?"

"I don't know, but they did," said Ben. "Proper speaking parts."

"And guess who got them," said Thomas.

Fee smiled. "You?" she asked.

Thomas shook his head sadly.

Now Poppy groaned. "Oh no!" she exclaimed. "You mean that ..."

She did not finish. "Yes," said Ben. "Hardtack and Shark. They chose *them*! Can you believe it? They chose those two."

"They pushed their way to the front," Ben explained. "They elbowed everybody else out of the way, and when the director said that he needed two people for bigger parts, they went right up to him and said '*Me, me, me.*'"

"I would *never* choose somebody who said '*Me, me, me,*'" said Poppy.

"I wouldn't either," said Fee.

"Well, they did," said Thomas. "And you should have seen Hardtack and Shark when they knew they were going to get the parts. They turned round to the rest of us and smirked. They had great big, greasy, disgusting smiles on their faces – the sort of smiles that say '*See?!*'"

Poppy winced. "I feel a bit sick even hearing about it," she said.

"Well, it gets worse," said Ben.

Thomas took up the story again. "Hardtack and Shark were told that they would be in charge of the pirates. That was us, of course. So they started to give orders: '*Stand here! Do this! Do that!*'"

"Awful," said Fee.

"Yes," agreed Thomas. "It was really awful. But wait till you hear this: after filming had been going on for a few hours, they brought us a whole tray of doughnuts. We were told that we could have a fifteen-minute break. And then ..." He paused to exchange a glance with Ben. "And then, Hardtack and Shark took three doughnuts each. *Three!* And that meant that we were four doughnuts short. Some of us had to share."

"Thomas and I shared," said Ben. "We had half each. Angela Singh only had a third, because she shared with two other people."

"Didn't they feel ashamed of themselves?" Poppy asked. "Not even a tiny bit? Well, I guess I know them well enough. They never do."

"They said that they were entitled to them," said Thomas.

"But they weren't!" Fee exploded.

Thomas went on to explain. "They said they had a much more difficult job, being in the bigger roles. They said that because of this they were entitled to three doughnuts each."

"But what about the director?" she asked. "Why did he let them do this?"

Thomas shrugged his shoulders. "The director didn't seem interested in anything," he said. "He just smiled when we complained about Hardtack and Shark taking more than their fair share. He simply said: 'You kids sort it out among yourselves.'"

For a while, everybody was silent as they thought about the injustice. Then Poppy asked Ben whether he had enjoyed the day, in spite of Hardtack and Shark. Ben did not answer directly, but seemed to be weighing up what to say. "A bit," he said, at last. "I suppose it was interesting – because I've never seen a movie being made before. But then there was something odd about it all. There was something that wasn't quite right."

"Why do you say that?" Badger asked.

Ben tried to explain how he had felt. It was difficult to put it into words, but he was quite sure about the feeling. He had experienced the "not quite right" feeling a few times before, and it had always happened when something was indeed not quite right.

"Because sometimes you get a feeling," he said, "that people are telling you one thing and thinking of something else altogether. Do you know that feeling?"

"I get it when I think somebody's lying to me," Poppy said.

"Yes," said Ben. "But it's not just that. I get that feeling when I meet somebody who … well, somebody who is just not a good person. Do you know what I mean?"

Badger nodded. "I think I know what you mean," he said. "I had that feeling in New York, when new neighbours had just moved into the apartment next to ours. I didn't like them, and I told my Dad, who asked me why. So I told him that when I saw them I felt a strange feeling up the back of my spine. A sort of tingling."

"I've had that," said Poppy. "I got it once when I was out in the bush. I suddenly felt a bit odd and shivery. We were camping and I was in the tent. And you know what? There was a snake curled up in the corner of the tent. I hadn't seen it, but it was there. It was one of those brown snakes."

"Are they dangerous?" asked Fee.

"Very," answered Poppy.

Ben was interested to hear more about Badger's neighbours. "What happened?" he asked.

"A few weeks after they had moved in," Badger said, "we heard a lot of shouting. We looked out the door and you know what we saw? The police. They were standing outside the neighbours' door and shouting to them to come out with their hands on their heads."

"And did they?" asked Ben.

"Eventually they were taken away by the police in handcuffs."

Ben asked what the neighbours had done.

"My father said they were Mafia gangsters!"

"So your feeling was right all along," remarked Poppy.

Badger nodded. "Yes. It was something about them."

Poppy turned to Ben. "Do you think your feeling is the same sort?" she asked.

Ben hesitated before answering, but then said, "I had that feeling when I saw the director. I had the same feeling when the cameraman arrived on deck. And I felt it, I think, about the crew of that ship – every single one of them."

POLICE! OPEN UP!
Ben asked what the neighbours had done. "My father said they were Mafia gangsters!"

"There was a snake curled up in the corner of the tent. I hadn't seen it, but it was there ..."
AUSTRALIA

GRRRR!
S.S. TOBERMORY
"Henry obviously had that feeling too," Ben said. "He growled when that ship came into the bay. He didn't like them."

"Bad people?" prompted Fee.

"Yes," said Ben. "I don't want to spoil things for anybody, but I think there's something very strange about that ship and those people. It's an odd thing to be filming such a movie here. Just think about it. Why would they do it?"

"Perhaps we should tell the Captain," suggested Fee.

Poppy did not think this a good idea. "What can we say to him? 'Oh, MacTavish B. has an odd feeling?' He'll just laugh at that. The Captain agreed to let us do this."

Ben remembered something. "What about Henry?"

They all looked at him blankly.

"Henry obviously had that feeling too," he said. "He growled when we met the film director on shore."

Poppy shook her head. "We can't go up to the Captain and say: 'The people on board the *Albatross* are clearly up to no good because your dog growled.' All dogs growl from time to time. He'll think we're half crazy."

"You're probably right," said Thomas, sadly. "I suppose we'll just carry on and see what happens tomorrow. After all, what other choice do we have? We only have these odd feelings and no concrete evidence. We can't accuse anyone of anything!"

The girl in the dark

That night, as they were preparing for lights-out, Badger asked Ben whether he had spoken to Fee.

"You were going to ask her about last night," he said. "Did she tell you anything?"

Ben told him about his hurried conversation. "She just whispered something and promised she would tell me, but not just yet."

"Not good enough," said Badger. "Saying that you're going to tell somebody something some time is just not good enough. It's just another way of saying that you don't want to tell them."

Ben knew Badger was right. He could tell Fee was reluctant to share the secret, and he imagined she was hoping he would simply forget all about it. After all, she had said nothing to him at dinner, when she would have had the chance to whisper to him without anybody hearing.

Badger, who had been preparing to get into his hammock, now stopped and sat down on a chair. "I think we should go and take a look ourselves," he said.

"Now?" asked Ben.

"After lights-out. Nobody will be around then. We can go and see what's behind that door."

Ben was uncertain. He had always been brought up to obey the rules, and he did not like the thought of breaking them too often. He had already done so when he went along the passageway that first time. He had got away with it then, but the more often you break the rules the more likely you are to be caught. If he was caught he knew he would be punished – perhaps even made to clean the heads.

Badger was staring at him. "You aren't scared, are you? Because if you're scared, then just tell me and I'll go myself. It's your sister and Poppy. I think we should figure out the secret."

It was a challenge, and Ben knew that if he refused to go his friend might think less of him.

He summoned up all his courage. "I'm not scared," he said, doing his best to sound brave. "I'll come."

It was not true, of course, and had he been Flubber, his ears would have moved as he spoke. But he was not Flubber and Badger seemed satisfied with his response.

They waited until lights had been out for a good ten minutes before they made their move. Badger had a spare torch, and he gave this to Ben so they each had one. "Don't turn it on yet," he said. "We can find our way in the dark, but we might need it later."

Keeping as quiet as possible, they left their cabin and began to make their way along the passageway. This ran the whole length of the ship, and they were only halfway along it when they heard the sound of footsteps. Badger seized Ben's arm and guided him into a recess in the wall. It was a place where a fire hose was stored, but there was just enough room to hide, if they pressed themselves far enough back.

"Try to breathe quietly," whispered Badger.

The steps had come closer and closer, and now, clearly visible in the semi-darkness, was Matron. She was busy carrying some bottles of drinking water to the sick bay. Had she been paying more attention, then she would undoubtedly have seen them. But, as it was, she walked right past, completely unaware of the two half-hidden boys.

They waited until Matron was well out of sight before they left their hiding place. Within a short time they had reached the end of the passageway and were standing in front of the door through which Ben had seen Poppy and Fee disappear.

"Are you sure this is the one?" asked Badger, his voice lowered.

"Yes," whispered Ben. "I'm positive."

Badger reached for the handle. Silently, with not so much as a squeak, the door opened before him. Inside was complete darkness, and so Badger switched on his torch, shielding its beam with his hand.

It was not an ordinary cabin – rather, it was a storeroom of some sort, about twice the size of a normal cabin. As the beam of the torch moved round, various items were exposed: a wooden barrel, complete with bung; a tangle of old rope; an open crate of lifejackets. There were also some stores of tinned food and a pile of spare deck shoes. It was exactly what one would expect of a storeroom on a school ship.

"Why would they have come in here?" asked Badger, still keeping his voice muted.

"Maybe they were meeting somebody," said Ben.

Badger shone the torch towards the back. "There's another door," he said.

They crossed the cabin. Ben hesitated, his hand above the handle of this second door. "Shall I?" he asked.

Badger gave him a nod of his head. "Yes," he said. "We need to look in there."

Gingerly, Ben turned the handle. Just as the outer door had done, this one opened easily and quietly.

Badger shone his torch into the darkness. "Oh!" he exclaimed. And then "Oh!" again.

Ben looked past his friend to see what was there. He drew in his breath. Then he too said, "Oh!"

Strung between two large crates was a small hammock. And on this hammock, covered by a blanket that looked as if it had been made of two floor-mats, was the figure of a girl.

When the torch beam suddenly fell on her, the girl gave a start and sat bolt upright. The expression on her face, revealed by Badger's torch, was a mixture of surprise and fear.

"Sorry," said Badger, automatically. "I didn't mean to startle you."

Ben looked over Badger's shoulder. He saw that the girl looked roughly their age, and was wearing jeans and a blue sweater. Her hair, which was long and dark, was tangled.

"Who are you?" the girl said, her voice trembling.

"I'm called Badger," said Badger. "And this is my pal, Ben. We're in Middle Deck, as you must be, I suppose ..." He did not complete his sentence.

"My name's Tanya," said the girl. "Actually, I'm in no deck."

"But you have to be," said Ben. He moved his torch away from her to illuminate the area around her bed. There was a kitbag and a small suitcase. The suitcase was open to reveal clothes, a hairbrush, and a few personal possessions.

"Don't you have a locker?" asked Badger. "Everyone's entitled to a locker, you know."

Tanya looked at him with wide, dark eyes.

Suddenly Ben understood. "You're a stowaway, aren't you?" he blurted out.

The girl turned her gaze to him. "Since you've found me, I might as well say yes," she replied.

Badger whistled in amazement. "You mean no-one knows you're on board?"

The girl now slipped out of her hammock and stood beside them. "Nobody knows," she said. "Apart from two new friends who have been looking after me, and now you."

"Are those two friends called Poppy and Fee?" asked Ben.

Tanya looked surprised. "How do you know?"

"I saw them," said Ben. "I saw them come here the other night."

"They bring me food," said Tanya. "They've helped me."

"Fee's my sister," said Ben.

This had an immediate effect. Turning to Ben, Tanya reached out and touched his arm gently. "So you're Ben!" she said. "Fee has told me all about you. She says that you're the best brother anybody could possibly have."

Ben was embarrassed by the praise, but it was something that any brother would be pleased to hear.

Badger brought the conversation back to Tanya. "How did you get here and why have you stowed away?" he asked bluntly.

Tanya looked down at the floor. "I had to," she answered.

"Who made you?" pressed Badger.

This question brought a sigh from Tanya. "Nobody made me," she said. "But if you were in my shoes you would have done exactly the same thing."

She was about to explain further, but suddenly stopped. There was a sound on the other side of the door that led back into the first storeroom. Tanya put a finger to her lips in a gesture of silence. "Turn off your torches," she whispered.

The sound grew closer, and then there came three taps on the door.

"It's them," said Tanya, still whispering. "It's okay. You can turn on your torches again."

"Who?" asked Ben.

The door opened and there, holding a torch, was Poppy, and behind her was Fee, carrying a bag. For a moment the two groups stared at one another. Then Poppy said, "Well, now you know, I suppose."

The bag that Fee was carrying contained Tanya's dinner. Ben recognised the contents: one of the apples from lunch; a piece of the pie that Cook had served up that evening; a slice of the cake they had been given for tea. There was also bread and jam, all wrapped carefully in greaseproof paper.

They all sat down in a circle as Tanya began to eat.

"You may as well tell them everything," said Poppy. "As long as they promise to keep it secret." She turned to Badger and Ben. "Do you promise not to breathe a word about this or … or …" She thought of an awful thing that might happen if they broke their word, "Or you'll be struck by lightning."

"We promise," said Badger. "Don't we, Ben?"

"Yes," said Ben. "We promise, or we'll be struck by lightning."

That was enough for Poppy, who urged Tanya to tell the boys everything once she had finished eating.

Tanya ate quickly, and with the last crumbs consumed, she began her story.

"I was born here in Scotland," Tanya said. "My father was a sea captain and my mother made flags for ships. She sewed these flags in our front room and then they were sent off to ships all over the world. She had other jobs too – she was always working.

"I had no brothers or sisters – it was just me – but I was happy enough. And then something terrible happened. My mother became very ill. She went into hospital and never came out. The doctors said they were sorry – they had done everything they could to save her, but she was too ill."

She paused, obviously upset. Ben gently asked, "So what happened to you?"

"Because my father was out at sea almost all the time," said Tanya, "I was sent to live with an uncle and aunt I'd never met before. They ran boarding kennels for dogs whose owners were away. It was far away from everywhere. I knew I was going to hate it from the moment I arrived. I saw that the dogs were not given all the food their owners had paid for, and were kept on short rations. The dogs didn't like being there and lived for the moment their owners came back to collect them. If only the dogs could have talked, they'd have told them the truth about that awful place.

"My uncle and aunt made me work really hard in the kennels. I had to clean up and look after any dogs that were ill. We had a little sick-kennel for them, and I was in charge of it. I didn't mind that too much, as I learned to help sick dogs.

"They weren't meant to make me work so hard, you know, but they did. In the morning I was sent to a horrible school nearby. I had always liked school, but not that one. When I came home in the afternoon, I had to go and look after the dogs until it was time for dinner, which was always cold and tasted horrible. Sometimes I was so hungry I even ate the dog biscuits.

"But every month they made me write a letter to my father. They told me what to say and they stood over me while I wrote it. I had to tell him how happy I was and how well I was being looked after. I had to say how nice the food was, although it wasn't, and I never got enough of it. I had no way to tell him the real story."

Badger was wide-eyed. "I would have run away," he said.

"That's just what I did," said Tanya. "I waited until they were asleep one night and I let myself out of the house. I took some food with me, and a bottle of water. I ran along the road that led to the nearest town. I was tired, but I made it. Then I hid near the train station until morning and the first train came in. I got on and had sat down in a carriage when I suddenly realised who I was sitting next to. It was the man who delivered supplies to the kennels. He looked at me suspiciously and then he went off to make a phone call. When we reached the next station there was a policewoman waiting for me. She took me back to the kennels. I told her I hated it there and that I was being made to work, but when my uncle and aunt laughed at this and said I was making it all up, the authorities believed them rather than me. That's often the way it is, isn't it? If you're young like us, grown-ups just don't believe you, even if you're telling the truth."

Ben was caught up in the story; he wanted to hear more. "What happened then?" he asked.

"I decided to run away properly, so I made a careful plan. I had read about the *Tobermory* and even once talked about the ship with my mother. I thought how wonderful it would be to go off on a school ship with a lot of other people the same age. But now nobody would ever send me off on one, so I decided to do it myself. I thought that if I was on the *Tobermory* then I might have a chance of finding my father's ship. I have no idea where it is, you see, and only my aunt and uncle know how to contact him."

There was something that Ben wanted to know. "How did you get on board?" he asked.

"You can't just have walked up the gangway," said Badger. "Mr Rigger always watches who comes on board. He would have stopped you and asked your name."

Tanya had an answer. "Yes, I knew about that because I watched what happened. You see, I had just enough money left from when I was originally sent away to my uncle and aunt's to buy a ferry ticket to Mull. Once I was there, I watched the *Tobermory* for a day or two."

The girls had heard this story before, but the boys had not. Nothing like this had ever happened to them in their lives, and they listened intently to every word.

Tanya went on. "I noticed that there was a boat that took out supplies. Most of the time it was tied up at the harbour, but every morning at ten a man would come down in his van, unload supplies, and then go out to the *Tobermory* where she was anchored. I hid in that boat."

"And then?" asked Ben.

"Because my father was out at sea almost all the time," said Tanya, "I was sent to live with an uncle and aunt. They ran boarding kennels for dogs ... I hated it from the moment I arrived."

"Then I hid near the train station until morning and the first train came in..."

Tanya smiled at the memory. "I hid under some empty sacks before the man came down," she said. "At times it was scary, as he put boxes and crates around me and I thought he was going to put one right on top of me. Fortunately I only had to put up with being squashed by a big bag of potatoes."

"But how did you get onto the ship?" asked Badger "That supply boat ties up alongside and there's always somebody on watch."

Tanya nodded. "I knew that," she said. "And so once the supplies man had tied up, I waited until his back was turned and I slipped into the water."

They listened agog. There was no doubt in their minds: Tanya was unusually brave.

"I swam round the other side of the ship," she continued. "You know that there's a sluice down there?"

"Yes," said Badger. "It's where they send scraps from the kitchen down into the sea – bits of food that the fish like to eat."

"That's it," said Tanya. "Well, I managed to work my way up that. It was just big enough."

Badger gave a whistle. "And came out in the galley?"

"Yes," said Tanya. "I came out all covered in scraps of fish and porridge and pizza crusts. The cook was asleep at the time. He was sitting in his chair, his arms folded over his stomach, his eyes shut tight. So

I was able to help myself to some provisions and creep out. Then I found this place."

"So that's how you did it! You were brave *and* lucky!" exclaimed Badger. But then he had a further thought. "How did Poppy and Fee find you?" he asked.

Poppy took over the story. "Henry," she said. "Henry found her."

"I wasn't cross with him," said Tanya quickly. "He was just being a dog. That's what dogs do, you see. They sniff around, and if they think there's something interesting behind a door, they'll scratch at it."

"Fortunately I saw him doing this," said Poppy. "If somebody else – one of the teachers, say – had seen him, it would have been a different story. I saw him scratching at that outer door, so I came in to investigate and there was Tanya, just as Henry had suspected."

Badger listened to this. Then he asked her what she thought would happen if one of the teachers were to find her.

"They'd probably send me back to my uncle and aunt," she replied. "They don't know, you see. They don't know what they're really like."

"And we can't let that happen," said Poppy.

"No," said Fee. 'We absolutely can't." She turned to Ben. "You and Badger agree, don't you?"

Ben looked at Badger. His friend said nothing, and it seemed to Ben that he was not sure what to do. Fee noticed this hesitation too.

"Well, Badger," she said. "I asked a question."

Badger's response, when it came, was mumbled. "I suppose so," he said. "But can Tanya stay here for the whole voyage? That's a whole term, you know. Three months."

"Of course she can," said Poppy briskly.

"And you'll bring her food for all that time?" asked Badger. "Every day?"

Poppy did not hesitate. "Of course. Why not?"

Badger thought for a moment. "What if Cook notices?" he said. "What if one of the other teachers catches you with extra food?" He paused. "We saw Matron on our way here, you know. She was in the passageway. She could easily have spotted us."

Poppy leaned forward to address Badger face to face. "Are you scared, Badger?"

Badger answered immediately. "No, of course not."

"Then stop inventing problems," said Poppy.

Badger was silent, but Ben knew that his friend was worried. Later, when they had all said good night to Tanya and had gone back to their cabins, the two boys discussed the night's events. They had rolled themselves into their hammocks and were waiting for sleep to overtake them. But it seemed that there was so much to talk about before that could happen.

"I feel really sorry for Tanya," said Badger.

From across the cabin, Ben said, "So do I. Imagine what it must be like having to live somewhere you hate."

"And having to work long hours," said Badger. "I thought that sort of thing stopped a long time ago."

"Some people still have a pretty tough life," said Ben. "That's why you still get people running away. It happens." He paused for a moment, remembering something his father had once said to him. *Try to imagine that you're in another person's shoes*, he had said. *The world can look very different that way.* His father was right: it was easy to say what other people should do until you were in their shoes yourself. Then it was just a little bit harder. So he said to Badger, "What would you do if you were Tanya?"

He had to wait for a while before Badger answered. "I suppose I'd do what she did," he said. "If nobody believed me, and if things were as bad as she said they were, I'd run away. But only if there was nothing else I could do, and nobody I could speak to. Most people have got *somebody* they can speak to."

"I'd do that too," said Ben.

There was something still troubling Badger. "But she's going to be found out, you know. She can't stay in that cabin for the whole term. She'll get sick. There's only that one little porthole and she can't have much light during the day. You get sick if you don't get enough daylight, and she'll need to wash and move around."

"I suppose so," said Ben.

Badger's voice betrayed his anxiety. "And sooner or later one of the teachers is going to want something from the storeroom. So they go in and what do they find? A stowaway. Then what? They find out who's been feeding her. They find out who's known about her. And who's that? Your sister and Poppy have been feeding her and we've known all about it and done nothing. You know what they'll say?"

Ben was not enjoying this conversation. He knew that Badger was right.

"They'll say," Badger continued, "that we should have told the Captain. They'll punish us all."

"Cleaning the heads for a week? For two weeks?"

Badger thought it would be far worse. "No, something much more serious than that. Expulsion. You know what that is? Being kicked out of the school. We'll all lose our places on the *Tobermory*. They'll sail to the nearest port and tell our parents to come and fetch us."

Ben was silent. He imagined the shame his parents would feel if both he and Fee were expelled from the *Tobermory*. His parents were kind, but there would be no hiding their disappointment that their two children had let them down so badly.

"Mind you," added Badger. "I don't think my parents would even notice. But I would, Ben. I like this ship. I like the Captain. I like Mr Rigger. I like Matron and I like Cook. I don't want them to think that I care so little for them that I can break one of the most important rules on any ship – the rule that you don't hide a stowaway."

Ben could think of no answer to that. So he simply said, "What do we do, Badge?"

He heard Badger sigh. "I just don't know, Ben. Maybe this is one of those times when you can't do anything. We can't have Tanya sent back to those people – we can't let her down. But we can't hide something that serious from the Captain. We're sailors, Ben. We owe the Captain our loyalty."

"So we do nothing?" asked Ben.

"Yes," said Badger. "For the time being, we do nothing at all."

On the movie set

The extras left the ship immediately after breakfast the following day, making the short journey to the *Albatross* in two small rowing boats. Both ships had spent the night out at sea, although they had remained quite close to the island of Coll, an island with a few small hills, dotted here and there, and some farms. From where they were they could make out the island's beaches – strips of inviting white and golden sand pounded by the waves that came in from the open sea to the west.

Ben and Thomas found themselves in the same rowing boat as William Edward Hardtack and Geoffrey Shark. They had tried to avoid this, but when you are lowering yourself into small boats tied to the side of a ship and are going up and down with the waves, it can be difficult to get things just as you want them to be.

They were all meant to take a turn at rowing, but Hardtack and Shark had other views on this.

"Sorry," said Hardtack. "Can't row. I need all my energy for my acting role."

"And I can't either," said Shark. "It messes up my hair if I exert myself."

Neither Ben nor Thomas said anything. They were both rowing when these remarks were made and they simply redoubled their efforts with the oars, ignoring Hardtack and Shark.

Hardtack leaned back against the side of the boat. "We're not moving very fast," he said. "In fact, we're hardly making any progress against the current. You guys should row faster, shouldn't they, Geoffrey?"

Shark sniggered. "Girls can row better than this."

Ben bit his lip. He was sure that Shark would never dare to say something like that if Poppy were there.

Hardtack pretended to yawn. "Oh well," he said, looking at his watch, "as long as we arrive before it's dark."

Thomas muttered under his breath. "Can you do better, Hardtack?"

"Did I hear something?" asked Hardtack. "Was that a seagull I heard, or was it by any chance you, Seagrape?"

"Yes, you did hear something," said Thomas. "And it was me. I said: 'If you're so good at it, then why don't you do it?'"

Hardtack snarled his response. "Listen, Seagrape:

you're just a junior extra – get that? Junior extra. If I report you to the director he'll send you back. So just watch your step, right?" He transferred his gaze to Ben. "Same goes for you, MacFish."

"He's called MacTavish," said Thomas.

Hardtack laughed. "That's what I said: MacFish."

Geoffrey Shark found this amusing. "That's right, William. You said MacFish. That's his name, isn't it?"

They were now getting close to the other ship, and the argument died down. As they approached the side of the *Albatross*, lines were thrown down to secure them to the side, and they soon clambered aboard. There the director was waiting for them, along with the cameraman and the woman with the two-way radio, who seemed only to run around barking instructions at anybody she saw.

It did not take long for everybody to get into his or her costume and for filming to begin. Once they were ready, the director started to call out instructions through a megaphone, telling people where to stand and what to do. It had seemed exciting work the previous day – mainly because it was so new – but now Ben found himself feeling a little bored.

Thomas felt the same. "I wish something more interesting would happen," he said out of the side of his mouth. "I've had enough standing around."

Geoffrey Shark, who was not far away, overheard this. "You'd better watch out, Seagrape," he threatened. "I'll report you if you say things like that."

"Ignore him," whispered Ben.

Ben wondered why they seemed to be shooting the same scene over and over again. He had heard that this happened a lot on film sets, but he had never imagined that they would need to do things twenty or thirty times. He noticed that a great deal of attention was being paid to a group of photographers and newspaper reporters who had arrived by boat from the mainland. They were busy taking pictures of everything that was going on, and were also conducting interviews. Hardtack had been photographed and interviewed six times, and Shark twice. Shark had been pleased to be photographed, and had spent a lot of time adjusting his hairstyle and working out which was his best side for the photographs.

Ben and Thomas had been able to listen to one of Hardtack's interviews, and had been sickened by what they had heard.

"I'm very pleased to be given this chance," said Hardtack to the reporters. "I've always wanted to show how well I can act, and now this opportunity has arisen, I'm glad to be able to take advantage of it."

The reporters had written all this down, and then one asked: "You're so young, Mr Hardtack, but have you any idea of your next role?"

The director started to call out instructions through a megaphone, telling people where to stand and what to do ...
CLICK WHIRRR CLICK
CLICK
"I've always wanted to be an actor," said Hardtack.
Shark grinned and preened himself as the cameras turned in his direction ...

Hardtack pretended to think for a moment. "I'm expecting offers," he said. "A few have probably come in already. I don't think I should speak about them. They're mostly confidential, you see."

The reporters had nodded, but Ben had whispered to Thomas: "They're mostly non-existent."

"They're *all* non-existent," Thomas whispered back.

"What are the challenges of acting in this movie?" asked another reporter.

Hardtack smiled. "Some people may find it challenging," he said. "I haven't, of course, but some of these extras ..." And here he pointed to everybody else (except Shark) before continuing, "They find it pretty hard. They're new to it, you see."

"Mr Hardtack," said a reporter, "What exactly is your role? What about Hollywood?"

Hardtack smiled again and made a generous gesture in Shark's direction. "Geoffrey and I will be talking about Hollywood," he said. "I'm sure we'll make an announcement at some point. My role ... well, I'm a star."

Shark grinned and preened himself as the cameras turned in his direction. Then the director, who had been hovering around in the background, stepped forward and brought the interview to an end. "Mr Hardtack is needed as we're about to start filming again. I would greatly appreciate it if you people could let him and his colleagues get on with things," the director said. "Thank you so much for coming."

The reporters and photographers were ushered to the ladder that led to their waiting boat. The director walked with them, slapping them on the back in a friendly way, inviting them to return again some time, and saying how much he looked forward to reading their articles. Once they had left, though, he returned to the group of extras and told them that there would be no more filming, and that they would be going back to the *Tobermory*. They should return their costumes first, he said, as he did not want the staff of the *Tobermory* to be alarmed by the sight of two boatfuls of pirates approaching them! He waited for people to laugh at his joke, but nobody did, apart from Hardtack and Shark, who laughed loudly.

"But before you go," said the director, "we'll give you a good lunch on deck. This is a thank you for all the help you've given us." He turned to the cameraman. "That so, Eddie?"

The cameraman smiled. "Yes, great acting, everyone! Fantastic!" He turned to Hardtack, adding, "Specially you, Snark."

"No, I'm William," said Hardtack. "He's Shark."

Ben suppressed a laugh. *Snark!*

"Whatever," said the cameraman. "Well done, Shark, and … er … Tack. Great acting, guys!"

The lunch took some time to arrive. Ben and

Thomas sat on deck and watched the cameraman dismantle the large movie camera. This had been mounted on a trolley, and the trolley was connected to a large battery block with a tangle of wires. The cameraman laid the camera on its side in an open crate, disconnected the wires, and then disappeared below deck.

Thomas nudged Ben in the ribs. "I want to go and take a look," he said, his voice lowered.

"At what?" asked Ben.

"At that camera," said Thomas.

"Why?"

Thomas shrugged. "There's something not quite right."

Ben said nothing. He rather agreed with Thomas, but he could not say exactly why he thought there was something not quite right. He was keen to get back to the *Tobermory*, but thought there would be no harm in having a look at the camera, which was now lying unattended.

Nobody paid any attention to them as they sidled over to the crate in which the camera had been placed. Thomas bent down to examine it.

"You know something?" he whispered to Ben. "This is just a much bigger version of a camera my uncle has. He takes wedding videos in Jamaica. You know – when people get married they want to have a video of everything that happens. He does that."

"So?" said Ben.

"I'm just saying," said Thomas. He leaned forward to examine the camera more closely. "You see over here ..." He pointed to the side of the camera.

"Yes?"

"That's the bit where the film is recorded. You put these high capacity memory cards in there. In those slots."

Ben looked down at the camera. He was not particularly interested in this, but it seemed that Thomas was.

Thomas looked up at him. "You know, Ben, this camera hasn't been recording anything. Those slots are empty."

Ben did not understand. "But why would they ..."

He was unable to finish his question. The cameraman had reappeared from down below and was walking back towards the camera.

"Just walk away," said Thomas under his breath. "Act innocent."

They strolled off, as if they were merely walking about the deck, taking a general interest in everything. The cameraman, though, appeared not to have seen them examining his equipment. He closed up the crate and bundled the wires into a separate box. Then he went down below again.

Thomas turned to Ben. He spoke quietly and without expression – anybody looking on would have thought this was simply a chat between friends. "I think this is all a fraud," he said quietly. "This whole thing, Ben, is for show. There's no movie being made – none!"

Ben kept up the pretence of the casual chat, but there was a note of real puzzlement in his voice. "But why?" he asked. "Why would they go to all the trouble?"

Thomas shook his head. "Who knows? All I can say is that I think the director is not a real director at all and the cameraman is not a real cameraman. And the two they picked as the main actors are nasty and never had many lines to say. Everyone just walks around in costumes."

Ben was thinking about Hardtack's press conference. The reporters and the photographers had obviously been invited to the ship. A lot of trouble had been taken: a boat had been sent for them and the director had made a big effort to impress them. It was clear that for whatever reason, the director wanted the newspapers to *think* he was making a movie.

Ben's brow knitted into a frown of concentration as he thought the matter through. If you want people to notice you are doing something, it might be because you do not want them to notice that you are really doing something else. And that something else might well be something that you should not be doing ...

He turned to Thomas. "They're up to something, aren't they?"

Thomas had been thinking exactly the same thing. "Yes," he said. "But what?"

Ben's gaze moved to the companionway leading to the ship's lower deck. Whatever it was the director had to hide would surely be down there. They had not been taken down below since they started filming – not once. "If there's a secret," Ben whispered, "it's down there."

Thomas did not say anything, but Ben could see that he agreed.

"So what do we do?" asked Ben.

Thomas looked pensive. "I think we should try to take a look."

Ben gave an involuntary shiver. "But they're down there. The director, that woman with the radio, the cameraman – they've all gone below."

This did not appear to put Thomas off. "We just wander down," he said. "Act casual."

"And if we're stopped?"

Thomas smiled. "We just tell them we were looking for the heads."

Ben was uncertain. He felt angry that they had been misled, but he was not sure that he wanted to take the risk of being caught snooping around below deck. If these people were up to no good – and there was now no doubt in his mind that this was so – then they could be dangerous. If only Fee were here, he thought. He had always talked to Fee when he had been in difficulty in the past, and it had always helped. Or Badger. In the short time he had known his cabin-mate, he had formed a high opinion of the other boy and he would trust him in a tight spot. He liked Thomas, but he did not know him so well, and he was uncertain what to do himself. It was possible that they both might do something reckless.

"I'm not sure about it," said Ben. "And anyway, what are we going to do if we find something?"

"We jump that fence when we get to it," said Thomas.

Ben suddenly made up his mind. He could jump fences as well as anybody else – he hoped. "All right," he said. "Let's go."

They made their way as casually as possible towards the companionway, the steps that led down into the heart of the ship. Although there was no sign of the director and his friends, there were several members of the ship's crew on deck. They were busy with the tasks of sailing, though, and did not seem to be paying much attention to what the extras were doing. Most of them were still enjoying the lunch that had been laid on for them, although a few were chatting to one another up at the ship's bow.

When they reached the companionway, Thomas gave a quick glance over his shoulder, and then made a sign to Ben. "Right," he said from the side of his mouth. "The coast is clear."

Nobody saw them. One moment they were on the deck, the next they were halfway down the steep wooden stairs leading into the heart of the ship.

"Where now?" asked Ben.

Thomas pointed to a further flight of steps. "Down there," he whispered. "This deck will be where they have their radio room and so on. We need to get further down."

"Why?"

"Because I believe that's where we'll find evidence of … of whatever it is we need to find evidence of."

Again Ben gave a shiver. "But …"

He did not have time to finish. Somebody had come up behind him and had grabbed his arm. The shock made his heart leap in his chest.

He spun round. William Edward Hardtack was immediately behind him, and Geoffrey Shark was behind Thomas, whose arm had also been seized.

"Well, well," said Hardtack. "MacFish, no less! What are you doing down here?"

"We're only …" began Thomas.

"I didn't ask you," snapped Hardtack. "I asked MacFish here. Well, MacFish – why are you trespassing?"

"We're looking for the heads," stuttered Ben, struggling to free himself of Hardtack's grip. "And let go of me. You've got no right to touch us."

Geoffrey Shark, who had been silent until now, sniggered. "You've got no right," he imitated. "You sound like a girl, MacFish."

Suddenly Hardtack slackened his grip. "You know that there are heads up on the top deck," he said. "They told us yesterday. So you shouldn't be down here."

Following his leader's example, Shark had also let go of Thomas, who was glaring angrily at his captor.

"Then why are *you* here?" challenged Thomas. "If we shouldn't be here, you shouldn't either."

Hardtack moved closer to Thomas, so that he was speaking to him just a few inches from his face. "You," he said, pointing a finger at Thomas's chest, "are an ordinary extra. My friend Geoffrey and I are proper actors. Proper actors can go where they like."

"That's right. We can go where we like," Shark repeated.

Ben and Thomas both realised that there was no point in drawing out this unwanted conversation.

"Suit yourselves," said Thomas, as if he did not care in the slightest. "Let's go back up on deck, Ben. The company's not so good down here anyway."

They turned and began to make their way back up the companionway. As they did so, Hardtack called out to them. "Did you guys see my press conference? Did you see all the photographers? How about that!"

"William's a star," added Shark. "And don't you forget it."

"And you too, Geoff," said William Edward Hardtack. "You were pretty good yourself."

Up on deck, Ben and Thomas went to join the other extras. Their boats had now been brought round to the side of the ship, and a member of the crew was helpfully preparing the ladders down which they would climb. Finding himself standing next to this crew member, Ben asked him when the movie would be finished.

"I don't know," said the man. "I'm just crew."

"By the way," said Ben. "What's the movie called? I don't think they told us."

"Search me," said the crewman. "As I said, I'm just crew. Nobody tells me anything. Especially that stuck-up director, always prancing around with his megaphone. What a landlubber!"

Ben laughed. For a sailor to call somebody a landlubber was about the biggest insult he could muster. "You don't like him?" he asked.

The crewman looked over his shoulder. "Who does?" he said. "Nobody, as far as I know."

Hardtack and Shark now appeared. It was time for all to go. As they rowed across to the *Tobermory*, Ben watched the *Albatross* get smaller behind them. They were close to the shore of a small island, and he imagined that both ships would anchor there for the night. He did not think, then, that they had seen the last of the *Albatross*.

Thomas evidently thought the same. As the two boys climbed up the rope ladder to the deck of the *Tobermory*, Thomas turned his head and said to Ben, "We have to talk to the others about that so-called film ship."

And Ben said, "Yes, we do."

Matron makes a suggestion

Once again at dinner that night everybody wanted to hear about what had happened on board the *Albatross*. Ben and Thomas told them about Hardtack's press conference, which led to grimaces and expressions of disbelief.

"How did those reporters not see through him?" said Poppy. "Aren't they trained to spot somebody like that a mile off?"

"They thought he was great," said Ben, shaking his head at the memory. "And you should have seen Shark trying to get the attention of the cameras, patting his hair into shape, smiling that smile of his, showing his teeth."

"Ugh!" exploded Fee.

"Yes," said Thomas, "it was terrible."

They did not talk about their discovery of the empty camera, as there were too many people at the table and the matter was too important to be discussed so openly. During a lull in the conversation, though, Ben leant across the table and whispered to Poppy: "Can we meet – all of us – after dinner? Somewhere private."

Poppy looked surprised. "Yes, of course. But why? What's it about? Not Tanya, I hope."

"No, not that. I can't tell you. Not here. But it's very, very important."

He went on to say who should be there. "Bring Fee. And Angela Singh. I'll tell Badger and Thomas. The six of us must meet."

Poppy agreed and suggested that they could meet in the cabin that she shared with Fee. Ben said that he would make sure that the other boys knew; Poppy would tell the girls. Badger, like Poppy, was eager to know what the meeting was about, but Ben did not tell him. "Not just yet," he said.

"Is it about that ship?" asked Badger.

"Yes," said Ben.

"You saw something?" Badger pressed.

"It's more about what we didn't see," said Ben.

"You're being enigmatic," said Badger, who liked using the occasional word he picked up from the mystery stories he enjoyed reading.

Ben said nothing. He was not sure what enigmatic meant, and decided he would ask another time.

Ten minutes later they were all in Poppy and Fee's cabin. It was a bit crowded, as the cabin was not intended to accommodate six people, but they all found somewhere to perch.

"What's this about?" asked Angela Singh.

Thomas tapped on a table. "Ben and I are worried about something," he said.

"That ship?" asked Poppy. "You're worried about what happened today?"

"Yes," said Thomas. "Ben, you tell them."

Ben drew in his breath. His father had once told him how to tell people about something you wanted them to know. *Start at the beginning*, he had said. *Tell them where, when and why. Then describe what the problem is. Then shut up and sit down. That's the way to do it – every time.* Now he tried to apply this advice.

"Today we were on the film ship," he began. "There was me and there was Thomas. And Angela was there too."

Angela nodded. "Yes, I was there," she said.

That was "where", and "when" too. Now he had to say "why".

"We need to talk to you about it because we think there's something suspicious going on." That was "why".

"How do you know?" asked Poppy. "Why do you think that?"

Angela now joined the conversation again. "Yes," she said. "That's exactly what I thought. I didn't say anything to anybody, but I just felt uncomfortable.

You know that feeling? You can't say why, but you just feel uncomfortable."

"That's exactly how we felt," said Thomas.

"But it wasn't just that," said Ben. "Thomas and I found out something really odd. You tell them, Thomas."

Thomas explained about the cameras. He told them about his uncle's camera and he explained about how those particular models worked. Then he revealed that there had been no memory cards in the camera on board the *Albatross*.

"What this means," said Ben, "is that they never filmed anything. They've set the whole thing up to get people to think they're making a movie, but they aren't."

"Then what *are* they doing?" asked Poppy.

"That's what we don't know," said Ben. "Thomas and I tried to find out, but we were stopped by Hardtack and Shark."

"They became friendly with the director," said Angela. "Very friendly. You know how pushy they are – always wanting to be at the front of everything."

Poppy looked thoughtful. "But why have they gone to all this trouble just to make people think they're making a movie? Do you think it's something criminal?" asked Poppy.

Badger joined in now. "It's bound to be," he said.

"But what?" asked Poppy.

"Smuggling?" suggested Angela.

Poppy shook her head. "No, I don't think there's much smuggling round here."

They looked at one another. None of them could think of any explanation, even if everyone was now sure that something strange was going on.

It was Badger who spoke next. "I think we should tell the Captain," he said. "If we've discovered a crime, then the Captain should know. He can tell the police."

Fee agreed. "I think Badger's right," she said. "We can't do anything ourselves, so we should tell the Captain."

There was a short silence. Ben had not expressed a view, and now everybody was looking at him. "You say we can't do anything, Fee," he began. "But why are you so sure? We could try to find out."

"You already did that," said Fee. "You told us that you and Thomas tried, but you didn't find anything."

"We did – we found out they hadn't really been filming," said Ben. "But we were stopped by Hardtack and Shark before we could find anything else. That wasn't our fault. If they hadn't been around, then we might have discovered more."

"Are you saying that because there are now more of us we can go over there?" asked Poppy. "Is that what you're suggesting?"

Ben had not thought it through, but he was starting to think of something. "Yes," he said. "We could go there. We could go in one of the boats. We could go tonight."

Ben looked to Thomas for support. The other boy hesitated, but then he nodded. "We would have to be careful, but I think we could do it," he said.

Badger looked doubtful. "What if they see us coming?" he asked.

"We wait until it's completely dark," said Ben.

Badger looked unconvinced. "Or hear us?" he added.

"We make sure we don't make any noise," said Ben. He turned to Angela. "What do you think, Angela?"

Angela looked uncertain. "I don't know," she said. "Maybe, but then again, maybe not. I'm not sure."

Ben turned to Poppy. "Right, Poppy," he said. "We've heard what everybody feels. Badger wants to tell the Captain, and so does Fee. I want to go and take a look, as does Thomas. Angela isn't sure, and so she's not voting – correct, Angela?'

Angela nodded. "I just can't make up my mind," she said.

"So it's up to you, Poppy," said Ben. "What you say will swing it one way or the other. At the moment we have two votes on each side. Your vote will decide it."

They waited as Poppy thought about the options. It took her almost five minutes – but then she was ready.

"I've decided," she said.

"And?" said Thomas.

"I've decided we should tell the Captain," announced Poppy. "It's safer."

Ben and Thomas were disappointed, but they respected the outcome of the vote.

"In that case," said Ben, "we should go straight away – all of us."

"To the Captain's cabin?" asked Fee.

"Yes," said Ben. 'To the Great Cabin."

Poppy knocked on the Captain's door.

"Enter!" called a voice from within.

Poppy went in first, followed by Ben and then by all the others. They saw that the Captain was not alone, but was enjoying a cup of coffee with Mr Rigger and Matron. He seemed surprised to see them.

"My, my!" he said. "A deputation? How many of you are there? Six. Well, to what do we owe the pleasure?"

Poppy, being the oldest, spoke first.

"There's something we think you need to know, Captain," she said.

The Captain smiled encouragingly. "And what would that be, Poppy?"

"Ben here can tell you."

The Captain transferred his gaze to Ben. "Well, MacTavish B? What is it?"

Ben swallowed. Once again he tried to follow his father's advice: when, where, why. He told the Captain of the discovery that he and Thomas had made of the empty camera. Then he went on to mention the unease that he and Thomas – and Angela too – had felt.

The Captain held up a hand. "Hold on, MacTavish. First things first. How did you know the camera was empty?"

Thomas stepped forward. "Because my uncle has one just like it, Captain. I know where you put the memory cards. There were none in it. I looked."

"And how do you know the cameraman hadn't removed them?" asked the Captain.

Thomas looked flustered. "I don't think he had."

"You think that," said the Captain. "But do you *know* it?"

Thomas shook his head. "No, I don't, Captain."

The Captain looked thoughtful. "You said that Hardtack and Shark spent a lot of time with the director. Is that correct?"

"Yes," said Ben. "They had main parts."

"So they might have something to say about all this," said the Captain. "What do you think, MacTavish?"

Ben looked down at his feet. He was not sure what to say. Mr Rigger now joined in. "Well, MacTavish?" he said.

"Perhaps," said Ben. "I don't know, though."

"I think we should get them in," said the Captain.

Ben was aghast. He looked at Poppy, who shrugged, but said nothing.

"You, Badger," said the Captain. "Run along and fetch Hardtack and Shark."

Badger exchanged a quick look with Ben. It was a look that said: I have to do this. "Aye, aye, Captain," he said, and left the cabin.

The Captain looked at Ben. "I know you and many others don't like those two," he said. "But they're members of our school, just like everyone else, and I must listen to what everybody has to say."

"Of course, Captain," said Ben. He knew that the Captain was a fair man and that he was only doing his duty in calling in Hardtack and Shark.

A few minutes later they arrived.

"You wanted to speak to us, Captain," said William Edward Hardtack, smiling in an ingratiating manner. Shark smiled too, showing his brilliant white teeth. *Just like a real shark's*, thought Ben, and gave a shudder.

"Yes," said the Captain. "Now, I've heard a report on today's activities over on that other ship and I thought I might find out what you two thought of things. Did you enjoy yourselves?"

"Oh, immensely," said Hardtack quickly. "Geoffrey and I had major parts, Captain. We had a lot to do."

"I've heard that," said the Captain. "Well done."

"Thank you, Captain," said Hardtack.

"And this director," said the Captain. "Tell me a bit about him."

"He's famous," said Shark. "He told us about some of the movies he's made. He told us he's won prizes for them. Oscars, even!"

The Captain nodded. "And this one he's making at the moment – what do you know about it?"

"It's about pirates," said Shark. "They're spending a lot of money on it."

"I see," said the Captain. "And did you notice anything unusual? Anything not quite right?"

Hardtack shook his head vigorously. "No, Captain, nothing. They were all good to us."

"So you saw nothing suspicious?" the Captain went on. "When you went below, did you see anything odd?"

"Nothing at all, Captain," said Shark.

The Captain glanced at Mr Rigger, who fingered his moustache thoughtfully. "Anything to add, Mr Rigger?"

"No," said Mr Rigger. "Nothing to add."

The Captain made a sign that indicated that Hardtack and Shark were dismissed. They saluted the Captain briefly and turned to leave. As they did so, Hardtack looked at Ben through narrowed eyes. As he walked past, he said under his breath, "You just watch it, MacFish. I'll hear if you say anything about my new famous friends."

Ben did not have time to reply – nor did he know what he would have said, had he had time. And once Hardtack and Shark had gone back out, the Captain cleared his throat.

"You did the right thing bringing this to my attention," he said. "But the truth of the matter is this: you have no evidence, not one single piece of hard evidence, to show that there is anything unusual going on. You can't be sure that the camera was empty – Seagrape has admitted as much – and what else do you have? A suspicion? A feeling in your stomach? I'm sorry, but that is hardly enough for me to act on."

The Captain watched as the effect of his words sank in. "And here's another thing," he continued. "We've heard from Hardtack and Shark that as far as they could see there was absolutely nothing to be concerned about. So at the end of the day, what am I to do? I really don't see any reason for me to act. Would you agree, Mr Rigger?"

Mr Rigger scratched his head. "I'm afraid I have to agree, Captain. You can't do anything on the basis of a vague suspicion."

The Captain did not ask Matron. She had been listening to everything, but had said nothing. Ben glanced at her, and she smiled at him – but that was

"Hold on, MacTavish. First things first. How did you know the camera was empty?"
"Because my uncle has one just like it, Captain. I know where you put the memory cards ..."
INSERT MEMORY
Mr Rigger scratched his head. "I'm afraid I have to agree, Captain. You can't do anything on the basis of a vague suspicion ..."

all. Whatever she thought, it seemed she was going to keep it to herself.

After the Captain had dismissed them, they all went up on deck to sit together at the bow of the ship. This was a popular place for groups of students to sit and talk, and sometimes Henry could be found there too, staring out at the waves in that thoughtful manner dogs have, hoping to see another mermaid, perhaps. He was there that evening, and gave a bark of welcome when they arrived.

"Well, that wasn't much use," said Poppy.

But Fee felt the Captain had a point. "What he said was probably right," she said. "We have no proof. You can see it from his point of view, don't you think?"

"Maybe," said Ben, grudgingly. "But what about Hardtack and Shark? Surely the Captain must know they're liars. And even if they told the truth, they were too busy being stars to notice anything."

"Especially Shark," said Thomas. "Did you see his teeth when he smiled? They always make me shiver."

"I wouldn't like to be swimming and see Shark approaching me in the water," said Fee.

"You'd just see his hair," said Ben. "It's like a fin."

They laughed, even though they were all feeling a bit low. Then Poppy suddenly pointed to the companionway. "Matron's coming," she said.

Matron had appeared at the top of the companionway, looked round, and was now walking across the deck towards them. "Well," she said, as she reached them. "How is everybody this evening?"

"All right, thank you," said Poppy, politely. Everybody liked Matron, especially Henry, who was wagging his tail enthusiastically to welcome her.

Matron sat down on a large coil of rope. "Listen," she said. "I can tell that you people are a bit disappointed. You hoped the Captain would do something, didn't you?"

"Yes," acknowledged Ben. "We did."

"But we understand," said Badger.

"Yes," said Thomas. "We don't blame the Captain. We blame Hardtack and Shark."

Matron smiled. "Those two are difficult, aren't they?" That was all she said, but they knew from the look in her eyes that she at least had not been fooled by their performance.

Ben explained that some of them had wanted to go and take a further look at the *Albatross*. Matron raised an eyebrow at this, but then she looked over her shoulder and said, in a lowered voice, "Why not?"

Ben stared at her. He was used to adults thinking of reasons why things *shouldn't* be done – here was Matron doing the very opposite.

"Do you think we should?" he asked.

Matron thought for a moment. "Well, maybe I

shouldn't. Maybe I should be more responsible, but I don't see what harm a little expedition would do. I don't like the idea of those people on that ship getting away with anything. I wasn't suspicious at first, but after what you said about the camera, I think we should find out the truth."

None of them could quite believe what they were hearing. Was Matron actually suggesting they should go?

"Would you come with us?" asked Poppy.

Matron hesitated. "Well, the rules say that the liberty boats are to be used only with the permission of a member of staff, and I am a member of staff, as it happens."

"So if you give us permission, then we can go?" said Badger excitedly.

Matron considered this. "Let's think," she said. "There is no rule about when the rowing boats can be used. The there is no rule that says that Matron – that's me, of course – cannot say to people, 'Let's go over and take a look at another ship that happens to be anchored nearby.' There is no such rule, I believe. Nor is there any rule that says that Matron herself cannot go for a row with a group of students."

They stared at her, each thinking, in one way or another, *What a star!* Even Henry, who could not be expected to understand what was going on, seemed to realise that something important was being planned. He was wagging his tail from side to side, as quickly as a pendulum out of control.

Matron looked about her. "Be discreet about it," she said. "But we shall all meet in about an hour, shall we say – after lights-out. We'll meet over there, where that rowing boat is." She pointed to a place where a line was lashed to the ship's railing. Down below it, bobbing about on the waves, was one of the ship's liberty boats.

"Does everybody want to come?" asked Poppy. "You don't have to, you know." But everybody did – even those who had voted the other way earlier on. In their view, the fact that Matron was coming changed everything. That made it an official trip – or a sort of official trip, or something that might just be considered a sort of official trip if looked at in a certain way.

There was a chorus of voices, each of them saying, in effect, that yes, they were signed up for the trip.

"Good," said Ben, and then to Matron, "Thank you, Matron. We'll be there."

It all happened very quickly

In Scotland in early summer, daylight lingers until it is quite late. For this reason they had to wait some time before it was dark enough to set off. But finally the last glow of the sun disappeared and the sea and the sky were joined in the same velvet black. Now the only light to be seen from the deck of the *Tobermory* were the silver pin-points of stars and, here and there, bobbing on the waves, the anchoring lights of boats in the bay.

"That's her," whispered Matron, pointing to a group of lights not far away. "That's their bow light up there; that's their stern light, and that's their mast. I can't see any other lights, which means they've all gone off to bed. They'll all be in their cabins."

"Just as well," said Poppy.

Matron looked about her. They had all gathered on deck. "Is everybody here?" she asked.

"I think so," said Poppy.

"Right," said Matron, still keeping her voice

lowered. "Now, is everybody still happy to come along? If any of you are having second thoughts, now's the time to say."

There was silence. Then a voice spoke up. "Would you mind if I stayed?"

Everybody turned to see who had spoken.

"You see," said Angela Singh, "I'm just a little bit scared of the dark. I always have been."

If Angela had been anxious that people would laugh or make fun of her, her worries were soon shown to be unfounded.

"That's all right, Angela," said Matron. "Lots of people don't like the dark. It's nothing to be ashamed of."

"No it isn't," said Ben, who was standing next to Angela. "Don't worry. Nobody minds."

Matron asked Angela if she would stay on deck and keep a lookout. "It'll be useful having somebody here," she said. "If there's any problem, then flash this." She handed her a small black torch.

Now everything was ready. Badger had clambered down the rope ladder to the liberty boat, and was ready to help people down to join him. Fee went first, followed by Poppy. Then came the other boys – Ben and Thomas – and finally Matron.

Matron waited until Ben and Badger were ready with the oars. Then she said "Cast off!" and the boat moved silently away from the side of the ship, the only sound being that of the oars dipping gently into the water.

"That's good, boys," Matron whispered. "Row firm and hard. In and out. That's the way."

It was no more than a few minutes before they saw the dark bulk of the *Albatross* towering over them. From down below it looked enormous, and they realised that it would not be easy to get on board. But then Ben spotted something beneath the bowsprit, the sturdy pole that projects out from the bow of a sailing ship.

"There's a net hanging under the prow," he whispered to Matron. "Over there. Look!"

"Well spotted," whispered Matron. "Row that way."

It was one of those nets that are sometimes suspended beneath the bow of ships to catch anybody who falls off. That can happen when people are attending to rigging and lose their hold, or perhaps trip up over an untied lace, or are not ready for the sudden lurch of the ship as it crests a wave. The net on this ship had sagged, and so by standing up in the rowing boat, they were able to get hold of it and pull themselves up. Soon they were all on the deck of the *Albatross*, their rowing boat safely tied to a handy railing.

"Follow me," said Matron, her lowered voice barely audible above the breeze that had blown up.

In single file they moved slowly along the deck to the companionway. This was where Ben and Thomas had gone down below earlier that day, shortly before being stopped by Hardtack and Shark. Ben felt his breath coming quickly, almost in gasps. Fear had that effect on him, and he was now afraid, in spite of trying to be as brave as possible.

He was not alone. Keeping close to Poppy, Fee wondered what would happen if they were caught. If these people really were criminals, as Ben had suggested, then they could do anything – perhaps even be violent. And for her part, Poppy, who always seemed confident and cheerful, found herself keeping as close as she could to Matron.

They crept down below, where they were in complete, inky darkness. Matron was using a torch, the beam of which she largely shielded with a cupped hand, allowing it to emit only a faint sliver of light. But this was enough to make out where they were going and what lay about them.

On the first deck below they found the chart room, where the ship's navigator would plot the boat's course. Then they found the radio room, with its transmitters and microphones, its dials and lights, some of which were still glowing in the dark.

Suddenly the radio cackled into life. "*Albatross, Albatross, Albatross,*" a voice said. "This is Shore Station Alpha. Are you receiving me? Over."

"Albatross, Albatross, Albatross. This is Shore Station Alpha..."
Thomas put down the microphone. "Out means he's finished," he said.
Fee tapped Matron's shoulder. "Somebody's coming," she whispered.

They froze.

"This is *Albatross*," whispered Ben to Matron. "They want to speak to us."

"I know how to work a radio," said Thomas, stepping forward. "Should I answer it?"

Matron said yes, adding that Ben should help by making a crackling noise in the background. This would sound like radio interference and it would help to disguise Thomas's voice.

"Shore Station Alpha," said Thomas. "This is *Albatross*. Receiving you loud and clear. Over."

And while he said this, Ben cleared his throat in the background, making a noise that sounded like airwave static. "*Ggghhh*," went Ben. And then, "*Hgghsh ghrrgh*."

There was a brief silence at the other end before the next transmission came. "*Albatross*, this is Shore Station Alpha. You are not very clear – please speak slowly. Have you got what you came for? Over."

Thomas looked enquiringly at Matron.

"Say yes," whispered Matron.

Thomas relayed the message, speaking more slowly now and with less noise from Ben.

"*Albatross*," came the voice once more, "this is Shore Station Alpha. Pick up further consignment from us the day after tomorrow. Two more captured yesterday to add to what you have. Can you confirm please? Over."

Again Thomas looked to Matron for guidance. Again Matron told him to say yes.

There came a final transmission. "*Albatross*, this is Shore Station Alpha. Filming deception worked. All local papers carried reports. Coast Guard not suspicious. No interest from police. Well done. Out."

Thomas put down the microphone.

They looked at one another and then at Matron, waiting to see if she could throw light on what they had just heard.

"This means only one thing," she said. "There is something on board this ship that they don't want anybody – particularly the Coast Guard – to know about."

"But what was that about two more being captured?" asked Poppy. "Two more what? People?"

Matron frowned. "I don't think so," she said. "Why would they be capturing people?"

Poppy shrugged. "Perhaps they're not after people; perhaps they're talking about something else altogether."

Matron pointed to the companionway that led to the lower decks. "Whatever it is will be down there," she said.

"Follow me."

She was about to leave the radio room when Fee, who was standing nearest to the door, heard a voice somewhere not far off. She tapped Matron's shoulder.

"Somebody's coming," she whispered.

Matron signalled for everybody to stand well back in the radio room. Gently, she pushed the door closed, leaving only the smallest gap through which she could see what was happening in the passageway.

Fee was right. Two men came down the passageway, one of them carrying a torch.

"I hate going on watch," said one of the men. "Standing up there when I could be tucked up in my bunk – I can't stand it."

"Never mind," said the other. "We'll have tomorrow off."

"Bow or stern," said the first man. "Where shall we go?"

"Stern," said his companion. "There are a couple of deck chairs back there. One of us can have a bit of sleep while the other keeps watch."

"No point to it," said the other, in a disgruntled tone. "Nothing to look out for."

Their voices faded as they made their way up onto the deck above.

"Well at least we know where they are," whispered Matron, making a sign for them all to follow her. "Keep as quiet as you possibly can."

Back on deck on the *Tobermory*, Angela Singh sat by herself, looking up at the night sky. There were no clouds, and fields of stars stretched from horizon to horizon. It was often like that at sea, far away from the light of cities that made it so hard to see the night sky. Although Angela did not like the dark, she felt safe where she was – leaning against a life raft, feeling the deck move beneath her ever so slightly with the swell coming in from the open sea. She wondered how everybody was doing on the *Albatross*: had they found anything, and if they had, what would they do about it? *Oh well*, she thought, *I'll hear about it soon enough – it won't be long before they're back.*

Those were her thoughts when William Edward Hardtack, accompanied by Geoffrey Shark and Maximilian Flubber, crept up on her.

"So!" said Hardtack, as he grabbed her wrists. "Who's this sitting up on deck when she should be down in her cabin?"

Shark shone a light in her face. "It's that girl," he said. "The one with the teeth. Angela What's-her-Name."

It took Angela a moment or two to recover from the shock. "Angela," she said. "And there's nothing wrong with my teeth."

"Except they stick out," said Shark. "And there are too many of them. Rabbit-face!"

"That's it," said Flubber. "Rabbit-face, want a carrot?"

Hardtack laughed, but then his voice became menacing. "So where are all your pals?" he growled.

"We happened to call on MacFish and the Striped One and there was nobody in, was there, Maxie?"

"Nope," said Flubber. "Very strange."

"So we put two and two together and concluded that they had come up here. But where are they? I ask myself."

"Yes," said Shark. "Where are they?"

"Boat's gone," said Flubber, looking over the side of the ship.

Hardtack drew in his breath. "So," he hissed, "your friends have gone for a little row, have they?" He jerked his head in the direction of the *Albatross*. "Over there, perhaps?"

Angela said nothing.

"Your silence confirms it," said Hardtack.

"We should warn them," said Shark.

"Our friends, not yours," said Hardtack, snatching the torch from Shark. "I'm going to flash out a signal, Geoff. How about 'Look out for intruders on your ship'. Will that do?"

"Yes," said Shark.

Using Morse code, Hardtack flashed out the warning in short and long bursts of light: short, long, short, short; long, long, long; short, short, long; long, he began.

Powerless to do anything to stop him, Angela followed the code. She had been on the *Tobermory* for a year already, and she knew exactly how each letter was encoded. That first signal, sent so quickly, spelled LOOK. Now he would move on to OUT, and he did: long, long, long; short, short, long; long.

Hardtack completed his message and then, from over the water, a dot of light in the distance brought an answer.

MESSAGE RECEIVED. THANK YOU.

"Hah!" said Hardtack. "That'll sort them out."

Down below deck on the *Albatross*, Matron had split her party into two. In the first group, which she led herself, were Fee and Thomas Seagrape. In the second, led by Poppy, were Ben and Badger.

"Now, we don't have much time," Matron told them, keeping her voice down as she spoke. "So I'm going to go for'ard with Fee and Thomas, while you, Poppy, will take Ben and Badger aft. Keep away from the cabins, as there will be people inside them, but look everywhere else."

"Do you know what we're looking for, Matron?" asked Fee.

Matron shook her head. "No idea, Fee. But that's what makes a search so exciting, isn't it? You never know what you're going to find."

They agreed to meet again at the bottom of the companionway in ten minutes. Then, with Matron giving them all a good luck handshake, they set off. Fee kept close to Matron, and Thomas followed close on Fee's heels. As they made their way down the long passageway, Matron peered through any doorways that were open, flashing her torch into the darkness once she was sure there was nobody about.

At the end of the passageway they were about to turn back when Fee noticed something odd. Reaching for Matron's arm, she pointed to a trapdoor in the floor. "Look," she whispered. "Look down there, Matron."

Matron shone her light on the trapdoor. "Interesting," she said. "Well spotted, Fee."

Thomas bent down to open it. The trapdoor was heavy, but when Fee gave him a hand, they both succeeded in pulling it up.

"Careful not to fall in," said Matron.

"I'll try not to," said Fee.

Matron leaned over Fee's shoulder and shone the torch into the darkness below. Clearly revealed by the beam of light was a ladder leading to the deck below.

"Follow me," said Matron, beginning to climb down the ladder. "But be careful. Hold onto the rungs as tightly as you can."

Slowly and very cautiously the three of them made their way down to the bottom of the ladder. It was dark down there, and the batteries of Matron's torch were beginning to weaken. But there was enough light for them to see that they were in a large compartment – as big as the mess hall on the

Tobermory – and that the walls of this compartment were lined with large glass tanks.

It was Thomas who saw it first. "Look over there!" he said.

They moved forward, the beam of light moving across the glass surface of the tank. And then they saw what Thomas had seen. He had noticed only a movement in the darkness, but now they saw much more than that. It was a great black shape, and as the light penetrated the tank, they saw a long body, a great fin, and a wide, open mouth.

"A basking shark!" said Fee. "They've captured a basking shark!"

Matron drew in her breath. "Look at its mouth!" she whispered. "Look at the size of it."

"I've seen a picture of one of these," said Thomas. "I've never seen a real one, though."

But Fee had. "We went to photograph some of these," she said. "My parents were doing research on them and they needed photographs. We actually swam with them while my father operated the camera."

"Swam with them!" exclaimed Thomas. "But look at its mouth. You wouldn't get me in the water with one of those things around."

Fee assured him that basking sharks were quite harmless. "They don't have any teeth," she said. "That great big mouth just has a sort of sieve in it. They use it to strain plankton out of the water. That's what they eat – tiny little sea creatures, so small you can't even see them."

They moved over to the other tanks. In one of them, swimming about in a lonely, morose way, was a giant ray, a strange-looking fish with great flapping wings and a long whip of a tail. In another, also frightened and confused in their glass prison, were two young otters. These playful creatures, who like nothing better than to romp about in the water and who can become fond of human company, were clearly pleased when they saw the visitors.

"They want us to help them," said Fee.

"We can't do anything right now," said Matron. "We need to get back to the others. Then we can report all this to the Captain so that he can do something about it."

On the deck of the *Albatross* it all happened quickly. When the men on watch saw the signal from Hardtack, they immediately made their way back down below. They had intended to warn the director, but before they could reach their cabin they saw Matron and her party meeting up with Poppy, Ben and Badger just as they were about to make their way up the companionway to the upper deck.

"Intruders!" shouted one of the men. "Stop where you are!"

Matron froze.

"Put your hands in the air!" shouted the other man.

Matron hesitated, but then she gave a loud cry. "Hurry, go! Make a dash for it, everybody!" she shouted.

No one needed any urging. Leaping up the steps, the *Tobermory* party pushed past the two men, knocking one down as they did so and causing the other almost to lose his balance. Then, with Matron waiting to bring up the rear, they ran across the deck to where their boat was tied to the prow net. Bundling one another over the edge, they scaled their way down to the boat and prepared to set off. They all did this – except Matron, who waited up at the top to see her students safely over the side before beginning her own descent. It was the right thing for her to do, of course, but also the wrong thing, as the delay gave the two assailants the chance to recover. Pounding across the deck, they seized Matron as she started to climb down.

For a moment it seemed as if she would escape their clutches, but they were just too strong for her. Hauling her up, they manhandled her back over the side and onto the deck. Matron struggled as best she could, but to no avail. She did manage, though, to call out to the boat below. "Head back!" she shouted. "Row as fast as you can! Send help!"

Down in the rowing boat, with Ben and Badger at the oars, confusion reigned.

"What should we do?" wailed Fee. "We can't leave her."

Poppy hesitated for a moment. They could climb back up in an attempt to rescue Matron, but if they did that they would probably all be taken prisoner too. And if that happened, then it could be some time before Angela realised something was wrong and raised the alarm.

It was a difficult decision, but Poppy had to take it. And she did.

"Cast off!" she called. "Ben and Badger – row as fast as you possibly can. We'll send help."

They did not question her order. Into the sea dipped the oars and swiftly the rowing boat cut through the water. Some distance away, Angela Singh, who had heard the sound of shouting drift across the water, peered anxiously into the night. Hardtack, Shark and Flubber were there too, although they were ignoring Angela and talking as if she were not there.

"I hope they caught them," said Hardtack. "Serve them right."

"Yes," said Shark. "They've asked for trouble – and now they've got it."

But then in the darkness they could just make out something moving through the water. As the rowing boat neared the *Tobermory*, the three boys realised that everybody was returning to safety.

"Oh no," said Flubber. "MacFish and the others are coming back. And they will have seen us signalling to the *Albatross*."

Shark looked nervous. "What can we do?" he asked.

"Make ourselves scarce," said Hardtack. Cowards never like to be outnumbered, and so they did what cowards almost always do – they sneaked away.

Now Angela was by herself – or almost by herself. In her excitement she had not noticed the arrival of Henry, but now she was aware of him beside her, his tongue hanging out of his mouth, his nose sniffing the air. He had heard the voices on deck and had come up to see what was going on. When the first of the party started to climb back up onto the deck of the *Tobermory*, Henry became excited and let out a welcoming bark. In his eagerness to see what was happening, he suddenly jumped up onto a railing, teetered there for a moment, then lost his balance, falling headlong over the side, uttering a long howl of alarm as he plummeted down.

"Look out!" shouted Angela.

Down below, Fee and the others looked up to see Henry plunging down towards them. For a moment Ben thought that the dog was going to fall into the sea, but at that moment a wave passed underneath the rowing boat and pushed it forward exactly to the point where Henry was about to hit the water. So instead of a soft, watery welcome, Henry ended up at the bottom of the rowing boat, landing with a loud and painful thud.

Poppy carried him up to the deck. He lay in her arms, whimpering, his body shaking with fright and pain.

They were all now on deck. Poppy laid Henry down and turned to Ben. "Could you go and fetch the Captain, Ben? Tell him what's happened."

Ben shot off, and while he was down below, Poppy bent down to examine Henry. As far as she could make out the main injury had been to his right front leg. The lower half was hanging limply, as if not really connected to his body. Poppy knew what this meant: the leg was obviously broken.

"What are we going to do?" she asked Fee. "Henry's leg will need to be bound up and set – and we must be days away from the nearest animal clinic."

Fee reached down to comfort Henry. As she did so, she remembered something.

"Do you remember what Tanya said to us?" she asked.

Poppy looked at her with annoyance. "This is no time to talk about Tanya," she said. "Henry is badly injured ..."

"But that's exactly why I'm talking about her," said

Fee. "Remember she said she had worked in those kennels? Remember she said that she had nursed dogs when they were hurt?"

Then Poppy did remember, and lost no time in doing what she knew had to be done. "Please get her," she said to Fee. "I'll stay here and look after Henry; you go and get Tanya."

"But the Captain's coming," said Fee, thinking of what would happen if the stowaway were discovered. "He'll see her and there'll be trouble."

"There's already plenty of trouble," said Poppy. "Matron has been captured and Henry is seriously injured. Another bit of trouble isn't going to make much difference."

It was as she said this that Poppy saw something that made her blood run cold. Over on the other boat she saw lights on deck. Then she heard the sound of an anchor chain being wound in. The *Albatross* was about to set sail – with Matron a prisoner on board.

A chase at sea

After a few polite knocks at the door of the Great Cabin had failed to wake the Captain, Ben resorted to thumping. This quickly had the desired effect, and a bleary-eyed Captain Macbeth appeared at the door in his blue naval dressing gown. A glance at Ben's expression told him this was an emergency.

"Give me two minutes," snapped the Captain, leaving Ben standing at the door. But it was sooner than this when he reappeared fully dressed and ready to rush up on deck.

As they raced up the companionway, Ben breathlessly told the Captain what had happened.

"We went over to the *Albatross*," he said. "Matron came with us. She found what they were hiding – and so did Fee and Thomas. But just when we started to leave they grabbed Matron. She told us to come back."

"Where is she now?" shouted the Captain.

"They're holding her prisoner," answered Ben.

They had now reached Poppy and the others.

"The *Albatross* has weighed anchor," said Poppy to the Captain as he arrived. "They've set sail."

The Captain peered into the darkness. It was difficult to make anything out, but Thomas, who had been watching the departure of the other ship, was able to point in the direction in which she sailed. "Their course was North-by-North-west, Captain," he said.

The Captain gave orders. "Poppy," he said. "Go and call Mr Rigger. Tell him to report to me and then sound the alarm. All hands on deck! We'll set sail immediately."

"Aye, aye, Captain," said Poppy, starting to move away. But then she stopped. "There's another thing …" she began.

The Captain had already seen Henry, though, and now he bent down to examine his dog. "What's happened here?" he asked.

The person who answered was at Henry's side, tightly binding the injured leg in a strip of cloth. It was no one the Captain had ever seen before, and for a moment he looked confused.

"The dog's leg is broken," said Tanya, carefully attending to her task. "I'm putting on a temporary binding. I'll have to make a splint."

The Captain frowned. "Good," he said. "You obviously know what you're doing, but …" He paused. "But who exactly are you?"

It was Fee who answered. "This is Tanya, Captain. She's been on the ship since we left Tobermory. She had to run away from her uncle and aunt ..."

Ben took up the story, "... who treated her badly ..."

"... and made her work for nothing," added Fee.

The Captain pursed his lips. "We'll talk about that later," he said. Turning to Tanya, he continued, "Can you look after Henry?"

"Yes," said Tanya. "I've taken care of many dogs before."

"Good," said the Captain. "You and Fee take him down to the Great Cabin. Stay with him there. Let me know if you need anything."

Tanya lifted the injured dog and began to carry him away. He did not growl, nor did he whimper, but licked her hand gratefully. Henry could tell – as any animal can – that this was somebody who meant him no harm.

The Captain took up his position at the helm. All about the deck, recently woken people took up their positions. Training paid off – everyone knew exactly what to do in an emergency like this – and within minutes the *Tobermory* had weighed anchor, spread her sails, and was moving away in the breeze.

At the Captain's invitation, Ben and Badger stood behind him at the helm, watching the compass and acting as lookouts. Poppy was a member of a sail crew;

they were pulling on the ropes that would tighten the sails and give the ship the speed she needed.

Mr Rigger paced the deck, his moustache blowing in the wind, checking that everybody was doing his or her job correctly and making sure the ship was taking maximum advantage of the wind. He knew it would be difficult to catch up with the *Albatross*, as she was a fast cutter that could outpace a heavier ship like the *Tobermory*. But he also knew that in a race like this, sailing skill counted for a lot, and there was nobody with greater knowledge of the sea than the Captain.

"We'll get them," he said to Poppy. "Don't worry, Poppy. As long as they don't give us the slip in the darkness, we'll catch up."

Poppy tried not to worry, but could not help being concerned that the *Albatross* would get away. She did not say anything about this out loud, though, as she always thought there was no point in giving up before you start.

They sailed through the night, keeping strictly to the course that Thomas had seen the other ship adopt. They had little visibility, but by looking up at the stars with his sextant the Captain was able to tell exactly where they were.

"You're never alone at night, you know," he remarked to Badger. "You always have a set of friends up above your head."

Badger looked up at the sky and saw the great constellations dipping and swinging above him. It took him a moment or two to orientate himself, but then he saw the familiar shape of the Plough and there, in exactly the right position, was the Pole Star. He looked at Ben. "I hope Matron's all right," he said.

"She will be," Ben said. "Matron is tough." He paused. "Have Fee and Thomas told the Captain yet?"

"About what?" asked Badger.

"About what they saw."

Badger shook his head. "Go and get them," he said. "They can tell him while we're giving chase."

Thomas was busy with the sails, so Fee came by herself and reported their discovery to the Captain. Ben and Badger listened attentively as they described the tanks and the sea animals kept captive inside them. The Captain shook his head sadly. "Poachers," he said. "That's what those people are – marine poachers. They steal these poor creatures from their natural habitat and sell them off to unscrupulous collectors. It's a big problem."

He congratulated Fee on her bravery. "You and Thomas did very well," he said. "There'll be extra pizza for the two of you tomorrow – if this all turns out as I hope it will."

When the first glimmers of morning light appeared in the sky, Angela Singh, who was a good climber, worked her way up to the crow's nest. This was a small platform, a bit like an oversized basket, at the top of the mast. From there she had the best view of anyone, and was able to look out over the sea in every direction.

"See anything yet?" shouted the Captain from the helm. Angela gazed out over the wide expanse of water. Although there was enough wind to fill the sails, the sea itself was calm, and there were few waves. At first she saw nothing – and signalled this to the Captain down on deck – but then, far away on the horizon, she thought she saw the outline of a ship. She rubbed her eyes and looked again. Yes, there was a sailing ship.

"Ten degrees off the port bow," she called to the Captain. "A ship."

"Is it the *Albatross*?" shouted the Captain.

It was, and a few minutes later it became much clearer. This was because the *Tobermory* was closing on its quarry, thanks to the skilful sailing of the Captain. By trimming his sails in just the right way, so that the wind flowed over them smoothly, he was able to coax just a little bit of extra speed out of the ship. But that was enough to make the difference, and within half an hour they were close enough to the *Albatross* to be able to read the name painted on her stern.

The Captain now sent out a signal to the other

Tanya lifted the injured dog and began to carry him away. He did not growl ... but licked her hand gratefully.
They had little visibility, but by looking up at the stars with his sextant the Captain was able to tell exactly where they were ...
"Ten degrees off the port bow," Angela called to the Captain. "A ship ..."

ship. This was done with brightly coloured small flags, one for each letter of the alphabet, that could be hoisted to spell out a message. STOP IMMEDIATELY, read the message.

A few minutes later, a response was spelled out by the *Albatross*, again using signalling flags. GO AWAY, this said.

The Captain smiled. "Run up the flags for N and O," he said to Ben. "They should understand 'No' when they see it."

Mr Rigger had now joined the Captain at the helm, and while the two senior officers conferred with one another, Badger was told to take the helm. He was a particularly good helmsman, and by skilful sailing he brought them even closer to the *Albatross*. Now they could make out people on the deck of the fleeing ship, and Badger was sure that he could see Matron, standing on the other deck, flanked by two members of the crew.

"There's Matron!" he called to the Captain. "I'm sure it's her."

The Captain raised his telescope and pointed it at the *Albatross*. "My goodness," exclaimed, "you're right. They're holding Matron on the deck."

"The devils!" muttered Mr Rigger. "How dare they!"

The Captain took control of the helm once more. "Well done, Badger," he said. "Good sailing!"

Now he explained to the two boys what he and Mr Rigger had decided to do. They would take the ship right alongside, up-wind of the *Albatross*, and in this way they would take the wind out of her sails. Once that happened, the *Albatross* would lie still in the water. "Then we'll send a boarding party over," he said. "I'll get Mr Rigger to radio the Coast Guard immediately."

Mr Rigger went off to gather everybody together, and soon the whole school was on deck. Everybody was excited and relieved that Matron had been sighted and would soon be rescued.

They were now close to the *Albatross*, and within a matter of minutes they were beginning to block the other ship's wind. When this happened, the sails of the *Albatross* began to crumple and flap and the ship started to slow down.

It was at this point that Matron made her break for freedom. Pushing aside the two crewmen guarding her, she made a dash for a nearby rope ladder that went up the mast.

"Keep away from that!" shouted one of the men.

Matron laughed. "Goodbye!" she shouted.

The men stood and watched her climbing up into the rigging. "No point in doing that," one of them cried out. "You're not going anywhere, you know."

From the *Tobermory* the whole school watched in astonishment as Matron climbed higher and higher up the rigging of the *Albatross*. With bated breath they saw her climb out onto one of the spars, and then, just as the *Tobermory* drew level with the *Albatross*, she launched herself into a high, graceful dive.

Poppy and Fee had come back on deck, and they both gasped as they saw Matron diving down through the air, her arms stretched out in front of her. And they gasped again as they saw her enter the sea, cleanly and neatly, causing barely a ripple in the water's surface.

And how they all cheered when her head popped up out of the water between the two ships and she began to swim towards the *Tobermory* with firm, powerful strokes.

Poppy and Fee were amongst the crowd of excited people who helped Matron clamber up over the railings. Angela Singh had run down below and returned with a fresh white towel, which she wrapped around Matron. Everybody was excited, patting Matron on the back and congratulating her on her escape. Cook, who had been busy in the galley while all this was going on, and who had missed the drama of his wife's adventure, was now up on deck, and he gave Matron a particularly big hug.

"You're all right, Rabbit?" he asked.

Nobody laughed. If that was what Cook wanted to call Matron, then that was nobody else's business.

Nor did they laugh when they heard Matron reply, "I'm absolutely fine, Honey Bunch."

Everybody was happy, but there was still a job to do. Mr Rigger had been down in the radio room and now returned to tell the Captain that he had been in touch with the Coast Guard. "They're sending a high-speed patrol boat," he said. "It should be here within half an hour. And in the meantime, they've told us just to keep an eye on the *Albatross* and make sure she doesn't make a dash for it."

The Captain knew that the *Albatross* would never be able to escape. Since the *Tobermory* was upwind of the other vessel, she would be able to prevent her from filling her sails with wind. The *Tobermory* was firmly in charge, and the director, standing glumly on deck, knew he could do nothing about it.

Ben and Badger decided they would go down below to see how Henry and Tanya were doing. There were still things to sort out, with what was going to happen to Tanya uppermost in their minds.

"I hope she's not going to be sent back to her horrible aunt and uncle," said Badger.

"I hope so too," said Ben. "But I suspect she will be."

It was not a cheerful thought to have on an otherwise happy occasion. Matron may have been saved, and Henry was in good hands, but it looked as if they would be saying goodbye to Tanya.

In the hidden tanks

The Coast Guard boat, the *Silver Salmon*, arrived even sooner than they had expected. With its powerful engines it made short work of the voyage, coming alongside of the *Tobermory* in a cloud of spray and with a triumphant roar.

"Ahoy there, *Tobermory!*" shouted the Coast Guard Commander.

The Captain returned the greeting. "Ahoy there, *Silver Salmon*!" he called out. "Come aboard!"

After the crews of both boats had tied large fenders, like giant inflated footballs, to the sides of their boats, the Commander was able to scramble across onto the deck of the *Tobermory*. There he saluted the Captain, who saluted him back, and then pointed out the *Albatross* wallowing not far off their port side.

"We've taken the wind out of their sails," explained the Captain. "They can't get away."

The Commander nodded. "What exactly are they up to?"

The Captain called over to Matron, who had reappeared in a dry outfit, none the worse for her dive to freedom. He introduced her to the Commander, who asked her to tell him what she had seen on the *Albatross*.

"They have tanks down below," she said. "They're full of sea creatures."

The Commander waited for her to continue. "Will you show me?" he asked.

"Yes," said Matron. "And can some of our students come too? They were there with me, you see."

"Of course," said the Commander. "They are witnesses, so they should come too."

Matron told the Commander about the radio message Thomas had intercepted. "That'll be their accomplices on shore," he said. "We've been watching a rather suspicious group who have been hanging about a disused lighthouse. That must be them. We'll pick them up later."

Word was passed to the group who had gone with Matron to the *Albatross*. This time Angela Singh was able to join them too, as it was now broad daylight, and although she was afraid of the dark, she wasn't in the slightest bit scared of daylight.

The Commander supervised everybody as they boarded the *Silver Salmon*, and then gave the order for it to skirt round the stern of the *Tobermory* and then go alongside the *Albatross*. As they approached,

Ben pointed out the director and his crew, who were standing glumly on their deck. "They know the game's up," he said.

"They wouldn't dare argue with the Coast Guard," said Badger, pointing to the heavily armed sailors who had taken up position on the *Silver Salmon*'s deck.

And he was right. When they came up to the *Albatross* nobody resisted the sailors from the Coast Guard, who tied the two ships together. Nor, when they started to climb aboard the *Albatross*, did anybody do or say anything. The two members of the *Albatross* crew who had stood guard over Matron, and from whom she had made her spectacular escape, looked particularly embarrassed as they watched the boarding party arrive.

Matron gave them a withering look, but said nothing. Her sternest gaze, though, was reserved for the director, at whom she shook a finger. Two of the Coast Guard sailors took hold of his arms and made him stand, under guard, to one side.

Watching this, Badger whispered, "If Matron has anything to do with it, he's going to be scrubbing the heads for a long, long time, I think."

Matron led the way down below. "We went right down," she said. "There are three decks. The tanks are on the lowest."

As they made their way down below, Matron switched on lights. All of the *Abatross*'s portholes had been blacked over, so that nobody could see in, but that meant that there was little daylight on the lower decks. Ben felt a shiver going up his spine. This was not a good place to be, he felt, and he was glad they had the Commander and the Captain with them.

They climbed down through the trapdoor and were soon in the secret compartment.

"There we are," said Matron, pointing to the tanks.

The Commander moved forward to the biggest of them. He saw the basking shark moving slowly within the tank, its great jaws opened wide in search of the plankton that must all have been eaten up by now.

He turned to the Captain. "We've been looking for these people for some time," he said. "We had a tip-off that somebody was capturing protected sea animals, but we were never able to find out who it was. You've solved a big problem for us."

"They told us they were making a movie," said the Captain.

"That's their cover," said the Commander. "I imagine that they thought nobody would be suspicious if they were filming." He paused, and smiled at Matron. "And they might have got away with it, if it hadn't been for you."

"Not me really," she said. "The ones who deserve the real credit are these young people here." She gestured to the others. "If it hadn't been for what they told me, I wouldn't have become suspicious myself."

The Captain looked thoughtful. "Well, they did come to warn me," he said. "But I'm afraid I didn't believe them. But now I know."

The Commander suggested they look in the other tanks. There they found the giant ray and the two playful otters.

The Commander was clearly angry now. "These people do a lot of harm," he said. "They take these poor animals from the sea and sell them to people who just fancy owning something unusual. It makes me furious."

"Me too," muttered Poppy, adding, "And sad as well."

"Yes," said the Commander. "It's very sad. But the first thing we need to do is return these poor creatures to the sea."

As the Commander was speaking, the Captain shone his torch up to the ceiling above the tanks. "There's a big hatch up there," he said. "I imagine that gives access to the top deck. We can hoist them out that way."

"Can we help?" asked Fee.

"Yes," said the Commander. "You people have earned the right to set these animals free. Let's start straight away."

The sailors from the *Silver Salmon* were experienced in rigging up pulleys. Once they had opened the hatch, they arranged a large block and tackle to enable the basking shark, which was extremely heavy, to be hauled up onto the deck. Fee volunteered to get into the tank to put the ropes round the great creature. "I've swum with them before," she said. "I'm not frightened of them."

The Commander looked dubious. "Are you sure?" he asked.

Matron supported her. "Yes," she said. "She's telling the truth. She really has done that."

It was a risky business, and at one stage everybody was worried that the ropes would snap, but eventually the shark was hoisted onto the top deck and then manhandled to the side of the boat. Then the ropes were pulled from underneath it and Ben, Badger, Fee and Thomas all pushed as hard as they could to roll it over the edge. Poppy was in charge of spraying it with water while this happened, as the skin of such creatures can dry very quickly when they are out of the water.

With a great splash, the basking shark fell into the sea beside the *Albatross*, its former prison. This brought a great cheer from the whole school, who had been lining the decks of the *Tobermory*, watching the amazing scene. Only three of the students were not cheering, and everybody on board knew exactly who those three were.

Now it was the turn of the otters. Once again, it was Fee who jumped into the tank to retrieve them. She had borrowed some thick gloves for the task, as otters can give you a bad nip if they are frightened or too excited, but these two behaved very well. Holding them carefully, she took them down the gangway steps and gently dropped them into the sea. As she did this, Henry barked enthusiastically from the deck of the *Tobermory*.

Finally the giant ray was hauled out, this time with the help of a large net they found on the deck of the *Albatross*. It was clearly relieved to find itself back in the sea, and as it swam off it did two great flips – rather like Matron's dives – to show its gratitude to its liberators.

Later that day, when the *Albatross* had been towed away by the *Silver Salmon* and the director and his crew were safely under arrest, the Captain left Mr Rigger in charge of the helm and went down to the Great Cabin. He had ordered the whole group of courageous students to report there, and they were already lined up when he entered the cabin. There was Poppy, with Fee and Angela on either side of her, with Ben, Badger and Thomas. Matron was there too, sitting in one of the Captain's chairs, reading a diving magazine while she waited.

"Now," said the Captain. "Are we all here?"

He saw the basking shark
moving slowly within the tank,
its great jaws wide open ...

Holding them carefully, she took them down the gangway steps and gently dropped them into the sea ...
ALBATROSS
SCHOOL SHIP TOBERMORY

He looked about him as he took his place at his desk. “No, I don’t think everybody’s here.”

Matron looked puzzled. “I think they are, Captain …”

He cut her short. ‘That girl,” he said. “The one who put the splint on Henry’s leg – where is she?”

Poppy gave a silent groan. She had hoped that with all the excitement the Captain might have forgotten about Tanya, but he clearly had not.

“Go and fetch her,” said the Captain to Fee.

They waited in silence while Fee was out of the cabin. There was so much that Poppy wanted to say to the Captain, but she dared not. She wanted to beg him to be kind to Tanya and not to send her away, but she thought that he would merely say no. Stowaways were always sent home – that was just one of the rules.

Fee came back with Tanya, who joined them in the line.

“Here she is,” said Fee.

“Thank you, MacTavish F.,” said the Captain.

He fixed Tanya with a stern gaze. “Young lady,” he began, “you do know, don’t you, that it is wrong to stowaway on a ship?”

Tanya stared down at the floor. She nodded.

“And the normal rule,” the Captain continued, “is that stowaways are dropped off at the nearest port.”

Nobody said anything.

"However," said the Captain, "rules can be applied very strictly … or not so strictly."

Poppy and Fee exchanged a glance. Was there a chance? Was there just the slightest chance?

"I have had a word with Matron," the Captain continued, "and she tells me that there's a spare place on board. I also spoke to the Coast Guard Commander. He radioed over to the mainland to find out if any girl had been reported missing. And the answer …"

Poppy gripped Fee's hand. *Please*, she said to herself; *please, please* …

"The answer was no," said the Captain. "Now, Matron has pointed out to me that this means that your uncle and aunt, Tanya, couldn't even be bothered to report you missing. Obviously I must conclude that you are not wanted by them."

"They don't care about me," said Tanya. "They'll be happy to be rid of me."

The Captain looked down at he top of his desk. He was a kind man, and the thought of Tanya being badly treated made him uncomfortable.

He looked up. "You were good to Henry," he said. "In fact, if it weren't for your skill in setting his leg, I hate to think how he would have suffered."

Again there was silence. Then the Captain said, "It's highly unorthodox. It's totally unusual, but I see no reason why we shouldn't admit you as a full member of the school. Would you like that, Tanya?"

Tanya answered, but nobody heard what she said. That was because they were all cheering.

Matron rose from her seat, crossed the cabin, and gave Tanya a hug. "Welcome, *officially*, on board the *Tobermory*," she said. "I think you'll be happy here."

"We'll try to find your father's ship," said the Captain. "We just might come across it sooner or later. You never know – the strangest things happen at sea." He paused. "Oh, there's one final thing. I understand from Matron that somebody signalled a warning from the *Tobermory* and that it's because of this that the *Albatross* was alerted. Is that correct?"

Angela Singh nodded. "They did," she said. "It was Hardtack and his friends. He took my torch."

The Captain frowned. "Fetch those boys," he said to Badger. "Tell them to come immediately."

Badger left, to return shortly afterwards with William Edward Hardtack, Geoffrey Shark and Maximilian Flubber. As the three lined up in front of his desk, the Captain looked at them severely.

"Is it true that you signalled a warning to the *Albatross*?" he asked.

From where he was standing, Ben had a good view of Hardtack's face. He saw now that the other boy's expression was one of injured innocence.

"Definitely not, Captain!" protested Hardtack. "We had a light with us, but we were just trying to see that everything was all right on the *Albatross*. We were worried about the *Tobermory* people who had gone over there, weren't we, Geoff?"

"Yes, Captain," said Shark. "We were really concerned for their safety."

The Captain turned to Flubber. "And you were there too, Flubber?"

"Yes, Captain," said Flubber. "And what William and Geoffrey say is absolutely true."

Ben's eyes were fixed on the back of Flubber's ears as he spoke. There was no doubt about it – Flubber's ears were moving.

The Captain looked up at the ceiling. "This is difficult," he said. "We have two different accounts here." He lowered his gaze, fixing it on the three boys before him. "I'm not sure I believe you," he said firmly. "I've been watching you, you know, and I'm not sure I approve of your attitude."

Good, thought Ben: more cleaning heads for Hardtack and his friends. And Badger, very much under his breath, whispered, "Expel them, Captain. Get rid of them once and for all."

The Captain stood up to announce his decision. "Against my better judgement," he said, "I'm going to give you boys the benefit of the doubt. It's possible – just possible – that you're telling the truth, and that there's been some sort of misunderstanding. I don't think you *are* being entirely truthful, but I shall, as

I've said, give you the benefit of the doubt." He paused, and then indicated with a quick gesture that Hardtack, Shark, and Flubber should leave the cabin. "They always get away with it," Badger whispered to Ben. "Always." "One day they won't," said Ben.

"They'll make a mistake." Fee and Ben smiled at each other. The boys headed to their cabins and the girls went to theirs.

Now Fee looked at Poppy. "Don't worry, Fee," said Poppy as they made their way to their cabin. "The important thing is that we rescued those poor animals. That's much more important than whether or not Hardtack and his friends get the punishment they deserve." Fee nodded. Poppy was right, and now, thinking about it a bit more, she decided that everything had worked out well. Henry was on the mend, thanks to Tanya's skilful treatment of his broken leg; Tanya herself was now an official member of the school and would have to hide away no longer; and somewhere in that wide ocean there was a happy basking shark and a delighted giant ray. The otters were probably on shore by now, playing around on the beach, as otters like to do. Everybody had reason to be happy.

That night, Ben and Badger talked to one another in the darkness, each lying in his hammock, rocked gently by the motion of the ship, pleased that everything had worked out so well in the end. The next day, they knew, was going to be a busy one, with more classes and with lifeboat practice too. There was always a lot to do on board ship.

"Are you pleased with life on the *Tobermory* so far?" asked Badger.

From the other side of the cabin, Ben gave his answer. There could be only one answer, he thought, and that was, "Yes, very pleased."

It was not a long answer, but Ben felt that it conveyed everything that needed to be said. He was very pleased to be on the ship, and he knew that Fee was too. And why should they not feel pleased? They were doing what they had always wanted to do – to sail – and they were doing it with people they liked – with Poppy and Badger, with Thomas and Angela, and with many other friends they had just made.

"You know where we're going after this?" said Badger, just before he dropped off to sleep.

"No, where?"

"The Caribbean," said Badger. "I heard Mr Rigger discussing it with Cook."

Ben closed his eyes and smiled. "Good," he said. "I'll like that."

A little later, he said to Badger, "Have you been to the Caribbean before, Badge?"

But there was no answer, as Badger had dropped off to sleep; he could ask him tomorrow, if he remem-

bered. Ben settled down. He felt his hammock swing slightly as a wave moved under the ship – a wave that had started far out to sea, and had come a long way.

Ben lay still in his hammock. He realised that he and his sister had much to tell their parents. What an adventure they had already had on the Tobermory. His eyes were closed, and he was thinking. *I have new friends*, he thought, *and one special friend in particular. We shall all be together, out on the open sea, for a good long time. What more could anybody want? Nothing*, he thought. And he felt Fee would probably agree. There is nothing better than being at sea with friends, with the empty sky above you, and the wind in your hair. Nothing.